TOWN ON TRIAL

Also by George G. Gilman and available
from New English Library:

TOWN ON TRIAL
George G. Gilman

NEW ENGLISH LIBRARY/TIMES MIRROR

for:

M.P.
a straight shooter
from Brooklyn

A New English Library Original
Publication, 1981
Copyright © 1981 by George G. Gilman

First NEL Paperback Edition March 1981

NEL Books are published by
New English Library Limited,
Barnard's Inn, Holborn,
London EC1N 2JR.
Photoset by Parker Typesetting Service,
Leicester
Printed and bound in Great Britain by
©ollins, Glasgow

0 450 04671 0

One

A WARM north-east wind had been blowing across this piece of west Texas throughout the afternoon. Now, as the sun sank and the crimson light of its setting faded before the encroaching darkness of night, the rapidly cooling semi-desert air was still. But everything, whether living or inanimate, that had been exposed to the wind was cloaked with the grey dust that the north-easter had raised, carried and allowed to fall.

Thus, the lone rider and his horse and the trail and the town marker were of a uniform coloration in the brief twilight.

The man riding the horse slowly along the arrow-straight trail had known for more than an hour that there was a town up ahead of him: had first seen it as a cluster of dark shapes which took the substantial form of buildings as the evening air cooled and the shimmering heat-haze disappeared. Then, as he rode closer, splashes of yellow lamplight began to show among the buildings – kept them from merging into the gathering darkness.

Night was fully born when the man reached the marker some two hundred yards short of the western fringe of the town: and was unrelieved by moon- or star-light, for in the wake of the setting sun, dark and menacing clouds had spread across the sky. So when the man had angled his horse to the side of the trail and reined the animal to a halt, he had to strike a match and lean down from the saddle to pick out some of the letters painted on the marker: and could not read all of them until he had used his free hand to brush dust off the sign. WELCOME TO IRVING TEXAS.

'Obliged,' the man drawled softly as he straightened in the saddle, raised the flaming match and lit the half-smoked cigarette that jutted from a corner of his mouth. 'I'm called Edge.'

The face fleetingly illuminated by the flare of the match was that of a man approaching forty years of age. Perhaps ugly or maybe handsome, depending upon the personal preferences of whoever viewed it. A long, lean face comprised of features drawn from the loins of a Mexican father and nurtured in the womb of a Scandinavian mother. The complexion was dark from a combination of his Latin heritage and exposure to the elements, the skin stretched taut between high cheekbones and firm jawline: and etched with furrows that were inscribed by the passing years but deepened by the harsh experiences of so many of those years.

The eyes were a light and piercing blue, and glittered icily between permanently narrowed lids. The nose was aquiline. And there was something cruel in the thin-lipped mouthline of the man. There was a day-long growth of bristles on the lower face: thicker above the lips and to either side of the mouth to indicate a Mexican-style moustache. Here and there among the stubble were areas of grey, but for the most part it was as jet-black as the hair on his head, which he wore long enough to reach just below the level of his broad shoulders.

There was no one close enough to take note of the face in the light of the match, but after the man called Edge had heeled his gelding forward and ridden in off the open trail, a few citizens of Irving did glance at him and his mount. And received a first impression of a tall, lean

6

but powerful-looking stranger. Six feet three inches tall and weighing in the region of two hundred pounds. Dressed in a low-crowned and wide-brimmed Stetson, a shirt, kerchief, pants and spurless riding boots. All looking as grey as the gelding because of the dust. There was a gunbelt around his waist, with a Frontier Colt jutting from the holster tied down to the right thigh. The saddle he sat was of Western style, hung with all the accoutrements that a cowpuncher would need to engage in his trade. Including a Winchester rifle in a forward-placed boot. And lashed on in back of the saddle was a bedroll and topcoat.

Nobody who saw the man ride into town bothered to give him a second glance for he looked much like countless other strangers who drifted in and out of Irving. Either a saddlebum or a hard-working cowhand between jobs. Grateful to get to Irving before the cold of night really began to be felt and the sky started to shed the threatened rain.

For his part, Edge appeared to give the town only a cursory survey as he rode along the centre of its deserted main street. While in truth his mind took careful note of everything upon which his slitted eyes momentarily settled. It was a no-frills cowtown which had sprawled out around an old Spanish mission. The adobe-built church was still there, fire-scorched and stained by time and neglect, situated midway along the north side of the street. And to either side of the mission and across the street from it were other adobe buildings which had probably once all been enclosed by a wall. But now they were merely houses and business premises of a different architectural design to the frame buildings which stretched out to either side of them.

Edge rode between private houses, some with front gardens and some not, stores stocking the essentials and the luxuries of daily living, a number of offices where specialist services were provided and then reached the bank of a broad, shallow stream. Where the street made a right-angle turn to the south, with buildings on just one side, facing out across street and stream to the undulating terrain that was spread to the east of town.

On the corner was a saloon called the Red Dog, a hotel named the Irving House, a building with a sign that proclaimed it was the headquarters of the Irving Cattlemen's Association, a small chapel and a courthouse. With the exception of the saloon, the buildings on this one-sided street looked recently built. All save the chapel had raised stoops out front and were two floors high. Immediately across from the courthouse a railed plank-bridge spanned the thirty-feet-wide stream and beyond this the open trail began.

There were a lot of shade trees in the town, all of them leaning to the south-west to indicate the direction of the prevailing wind in this part of the country. The stream made pleasant sounds running over the rocky bed and the water showed white in some places through the timber that flourished along the bank. The faltering music of a pump organ and women singing hymns came from the chapel. One of the four horses already at the rail out front of the Red Dog vented an ill-tempered whinny when Edge dismounted and hitched the gelding there. A middle-aged man with a bald head and a paunchy belly who was taking the evening air from the threshold of the hotel greeted:

'Evenin', stranger. Gonna have some rain, looks like.'

The half-breed took off his hat, knocked it twice against his palm and blew through the disturbed dust as he put the Stetson back on his head.

'It's my whistle needs wetting right now, feller.'

The man, who was dressed in a dark suit and white shirt with a bootlace necktie, licked his fat lips and nodded as he folded his arms. 'You're goin' to the right place, stranger. Rusty Donnelly keeps his beer cool and he don't water the whiskey. Passin' through or stoppin' over?'

Edge stepped up on to the stoop and paused to ask: 'You run your business as well as Donnelly runs his?'

'Clean bed in a clean room plus three square meals a day, stranger. A buck and a half. Bath ten cents extra. A man wants anythin' else extra he brings it into town from outside and he takes a room at the Red Dog. I don't rent double rooms to single men. No offence.'

'You got a livery, feller?'

'No, sir. But there's a stable on Lone Star Street. Jake Huber'll charge you fifty cents a night for a good service. I'll have my boy take your horse over to Jake's if you like.'

'Obliged.'

'Soon as choir practice is through. My boy plays the organ.'

With one hand hooked over the top of a batwing door, Edge cocked his head to the side and listened to the discordant organ music and off-key singing for a moment or so. Then grinned with his mouth as he dropped the dead cigarette stub on the stoop and said: 'Long as they ain't aiming to reach perfection tonight.'

The hotelman sighed. 'Joel is young. Willin' to learn but with more appreciation of one of the choir members than for music, I'm afraid.'

He grimaced as three discords in a row caused the women to halt the singing again.

'Maybe he'll strike the right note with the girl, feller,' Edge offered.

The man in the hotel doorway grinned as a beat was counted and the hymn singing began again. 'One good thing to be said for that, stranger. Joel wouldn't be able to play that danged instrument at his own weddin'.'

Edge pushed through the batwings and came to a halt, the doors banging closed against his back: as a man snarled:

'I told you already, Warford! Leave the lady be!'

Which was countered with a softly rasped: 'Mind your own damn business, Rusty!'

The saloon was longer than it was broad, maybe thirty feet by fifty. With the bar counter stretching three-quarters of the way down the wall to the left of where Edge stood. There were a dozen chair-ringed tables in the L-shaped area on the customers' side of the bar and a bare entertainments platform at the far end. The floor, ceiling and walls were untreated timber. Six kerosene lamps hung from the ceiling but only two were lit: these at the front of the saloon so that much of the rear area was in semi-darkness.

It was down there that the woman was seated at a table close to the bar, with a coffee pot and a cup in front of her. A slim, youngish, good-looking blonde, Edge thought after glimpsing her before she was obscured by the man going toward her. A man who had risen from a table directly beneath one of the lighted lamps. A table where he and three others had been playing cards and drinking whiskey. Donnelly was midway along his bar, behind it: closer to the woman than the advancing man.

'Play cards, Dean.'

'She give you the brush, kid.'

'Shit, I knew they'd be trouble.'

The trio of men at the table were all in the thirty-to-forty age group, which made them from five to fifteen years older than Warford. Rough-hewn men with sun-burnished faces and work-toughened hands. Dressed in check shirts and denim pants, scuffed boots and sweat-stained hats. Carrying Colts in hip holsters.

Tired-looking men whose weariness was suddenly jolted out of them by fear.

Rusty Donnelly also appeared tired as he became rigid behind his bar, hands splayed on the counter top. But he had that kind of long, thin, sunken-eyed face which would appear haggard no matter what the situation or his feelings about it.

'There's not gonna be any trouble in my place!' Donnelly insisted, bringing his anger under tight control. 'Go back to your friends, Warford.'

'I told you! I told you not to have her in here, boy! But you wouldn't listen to your—'

'Quit it, Ma!' Donnelly snapped, taking his sunken eyes away from Warford for part of a second to snatch a look toward a shadowed doorway from which the woman had berated him.

'All right, I'll go!' This from the woman at the table as she rose to her feet.

'You don't have to if you don't want to, miss,' Donnelly assured as Dean Warford came to a halt and stared fixedly at the slim-bodied blonde who had picked up a carpetbag from the floor and a hat from another chair at her table. 'It ain't you that's makin' trouble.'

'Just causin' it!' Mrs Donnelly growled from the darkened doorway at the far end of the bar.

The younger woman ignored the noise as she started away from the table but was able to take only five paces before her path was blocked by the tall and broadly-built Dean Warford. Who placed his splayed hands on his hips and rasped:

'Just who the hell do you think you are? Treatin' me like I was a handful of dirt!'

'If you were merely a handful, *sonny*,' she answered icily, stressing the implied insult, 'I'd be able to brush you aside. 'But it seems you are one big clod and—'

'Why you—'

'Don't, Rusty!' Mrs Donnelly shrieked and lunged out of the doorway.

'Watch out, Dean!' one of the men at the table yelled at the same time.

Warford had jerked his right hand away from his hip: up and across the front of his body – obviously intent upon landing a back-handed blow on the woman's face.

She stood her ground and simply squeezed her eyes closed and compressed her lips in expectation of the hand cracking into her cheek.

All this as Rusty Donnelly dropped into a half-crouch behind the bar, hands leaving the counter top. Then straightened, holding a double-barrel shotgun.

'Warford!' the bartender yelled, and began to thumb back the hammers.

But the act was never completed. For Dean Warford had seen the start of Donnelly's move before the bartender's mother and one of the men at the table shouted. And his right hand dropped to his holster and drew, cocked and levelled the Colt in a blur of speed. Then he triggered a shot from the gun a split second after his left hand sent the blonde staggering out of the line of fire.

The haggard-faced Donnelly got his nick-name from the rust-coloured mop of curly hair. Which in a few moments took on a brighter and deeper hue: as Warford fanned the hammer of his Army Colt to explode all six bullets from the chambers. Only the first three shells dug into Donnelly's shocked face, to tunnel through flesh and tissue and teeth and eyes and bones. To burst clear at the back of his head amid sprays of blood. This blood splashed against the wall into which Donnelly was slammed by the impact of the bullets. Then it spattered into the dead man's hair as the corpse slid down the wall. This as the second three bullets exploded from Warford's gun were imbedded with the first three in the crimson stained wall, after the eyeless face with the blood-filled mouth had sunk below the level of the counter top.

12

Gunsmoke drifted, its acrid taint strong in the air.

Choir practice came to an abrupt end.

The blonde made a moist sound in her throat as she continued to lean like a statue against a chairback where the shove in the belly from Warford had sent her.

The three men who had been playing cards with Warford were also rigid, but silent through the stretched seconds which followed the firing of the final shot.

The same as the grossly fat, grey-haired elderly woman who had emerged from the doorway behind the bar when she shouted the last words her son was ever to hear from her.

And Dean Warford, who seemed to be petrified in the half-turned, slightly crouched, arms-extended attitude of fanning his revolver.

Until the man called Edge stepped away from the batwing doors and said evenly:

'Let's start the wake. Figure with a name like Donnelly . . .'

Warford whirled: levelled his Colt at the half-breed. While the others snapped their heads around to stare at him.

'. . . he had some Irish in him,' Edge continued, eyeing the dead man's mother as he angled toward the bar counter. 'Me, I'm a rye feller.'

Two

WARFORD'S good-looking, clean-shaven, green-eyed, weak-jawed face was still expressing the remnants of fervent rage. And spittle spilled from the corners of his mouth when he snarled:

'Beat it, bummer!'

The other customers in the Red Dog saloon continued to be in the grip of shock. Which was abruptly deepened and in some cases was vented in choked gasps when the tall, lean, impassive-faced stranger responded to the young killer's command.

Edge's Colt came clear of the holster with smooth speed. But Warford's was already drawn and levelled. So the younger man had time to fan the hammer of his gun, stare down at it and then return his abruptly frightened gaze to the half-breed after the pin had fallen ineffectually against expended cartridge cases. And his fear expanded rather than faded when he saw that Edge was using the foresight of the Colt to scratch his bristled jawline. For the slitted blue eyes showed a glinting coldness which in combination with the cruel set of the thin lips seemed to personify a brand of evil that went beyond the bounds of human emotion.

Everyone in the dimly lit saloon witnessed the expression as Warford croaked:

'It's empty, mister.'

'That's what I thought about a gun that made my kid brother a cripple, feller,' Edge answered evenly. 'Reason I object to having guns aimed at me. You do it again, make sure it's loaded and that you kill me. Or I'll sure enough kill you. Everyone here heard that, so you won't get no second chance. Toss it away, feller. High.'

'Yeah, sure. Here.'

Warford threw the Colt with a sideways flick of the wrist. And Edge brought his down from his face. Exploded two shots. Each causing a shudder to wrack the bodies of the customers in the Red Dog and the group of bystanders who had been drawn to the doorway and windows of the saloon by the earlier, more damaging gunfire.

The first shot struck Warford's Colt while it was in the air. The second kicked it off the table top where it landed and clattered it to the floor at the base of a wall.

Eyes followed the jerked progress of the gun. Then returned to Edge and saw that he had tilted his own revolver: watched in tense silence as he ejected the spent cases to the floor and pushed fresh rounds into the smoking chambers before he slid the gun back in the holster.

The evil killer-glint had gone from the narrowed eyes under their hooded lids now: as he closed with the bar counter and swung lithely over its polished top.

Nobody said a word and it was almost as if they were all holding their breath while the half-breed brought a bottle of whiskey and a shot glass from underneath and placed them on top of the counter. The stream made rushing sounds along its rocky bed. Then a rain squall beat at timber and glass. Edge came over the bar counter as smoothly as the first time, took a five-dollar bill from a hip pocket and laid it on the top.

'A bummer I ain't, ma'am,' he said to the shocked Mrs Donnelly. 'I pay for what I have or if I can't I don't have it. You can make change after you've made the arrangements.'

He picked up the bottle and glass and on his way to a table on the fringe of the light and dark of the saloon he extracted the cork with his teeth and spat it on the floor.

Mrs Donnelly covered her fleshy face with both hands as her obese frame was shaken by dry sobs.

'You're a cold-hearted sonofabitch, mister!' the eldest of the card players accused sourly as Edge dropped into a chair and poured whiskey into the glass.

'I am what I am, feller,' the half-breed answered. 'And it's been a long time since I needed anybody to like it.'

'What's this all about?' a man demanded from the doorway. The one who had greeted Edge from the threshold of the hotel. He came through the batwings closely followed by a kid of about eighteen.

Those who remained out on the stoop, at the doorway and windows, were all women and girls.

'Dean just blasted Rusty,' one of the card players answered and drew a noisy response of gasps, shrieks and questions.

'In self defence!' Warford yelled. 'I got witnesses!'

'That's right, Mr Pepper!'

'We seen it all! Rusty was gonna use his scatter-gun on Dean!'

'Save it!' Pepper snapped and waved a hand at his son. 'Go get Wes Wilde, Joel.' He went to the bar, leaned over it and grimaced at the sight of the bloody-faced Donnelly. 'And Stan Barlow'll be needed as well, Joel.'

Edge finished his first drink with two swallows and then refilled the glass: nursed it at a sip at a time. This while activity increased, subsided, had a resurgence and then faded again in front of him.

His response to the levelled gun of the angry young cowpuncher had been a stupid waste of time, feelings and bullets. Normally when a man pointed a gun at him for the first time it was necessary only to warn him not to do it again.

And this aversion to looking down the muzzle of a gun had its roots in the truthful incident he had related to the people in the Red Dog saloon. He really had once had a kid brother – named Jamie – who he had maimed in a childhood game with a Starr rifle they both thought had no bullet in the breech.

Jamie did not live for too many years after he was crippled. Was brutally tortured and then murdered by six men who served under the command of Josiah C. Hedges, Union cavalry lieutenant during the War Between the States. That was the given and family name of the man called Edge in his youth and through the years of the harsh and bloody civil war. For he did not become Edge until he had tracked down and taken his revenge against the former troopers who killed Jamie and burned the brothers' farmstead on the Iowa prairie.

He used war-taught skills to accomplish his mission of vengeance, which in peacetime placed him outside the law. And the mispronounciation of the name Hedges by a Mexican had given him an alias which he had clung to even after an incident in the city of New York for which he had been granted amnesty on the old killings.

With the new name, he had not adopted a fresh identity: had merely reverted to the kind of man that he had become during the war. Which was not his intention when he rode westwards after the peace-signing at Appomattox Court House: for at that time it was his ambition to forget the harsh lessons of war and take up again the hard but peaceful life of a prairie farmer.

But the horrifying death of Jamie and the burning of the family home had dashed such hopes. And once the killers of the boy were as dead as their victim, destiny set a course of violence which the man now called Edge was bound to follow.

On occasion during the early years of following the violent trails laid out for him, he sought to spit in the eye of his ruling fates. To settle down, alone or with a woman, in some place where there seemed a chance of establishing a life for himself that might have some resemblance to the kind he had envisaged on the Iowa farmstead. But always his plans were ruined and his hopes were dashed: in a welter of flying bullets, drifting gunsmoke and spraying blood. Until regret, remorse and grief had taken on the sourness of self-pity, at which time he surrendered to his destiny. And became a drifter across the varied landscape of the states and territories of his native country and the northern regions of his father's homeland. Moving as need or the mood took him, living by a self-imposed code that demanded he accepted nothing from any man unless he paid a fair price: and looking for trouble only when he was engaged in a line of work that attracted it.

Like recently, in and around the Territory of Arizona-Mexico border-town of Indian Hill where he had seen an opportunity to boost his bankroll from a kidnapping that was none of his business. He went into that with his eyes open and therefore could have no complaint – and could lay no blame upon his ruling fates – about the way it turned out.

But arriving at the outwardly peaceful Texas town of Irving, coming into a saloon for a drink and getting mixed up in a killing . . . Shit, that was another matter. And he needed the shots of rye whiskey in the peace of his own company to keep from the futile mental exercise of cursing the twist of fate that had led him to the Red Dog saloon at the moment when fresh violence erupted. While at the same time he could congratulate himself for shooting at an inanimate empty gun instead of blasting a shot into the drunken hot-head who had aimed it at him. And be thankful this latest turn of events had not riled him enough so that he failed to realise – the way Warford had – that the gun was empty.

'All right, stranger. Now we get to you. What's your account of what happened here this evenin'?'

Edge looked up from the fourth glass of whiskey which he was holding in both brown-skinned hands resting on the table. And saw the man who spoke to him was about fifty, with a medium height and build: sporting a neatly-trimmed moustache and beard that was black mottled with grey. The face above the hirsute growth was dark-stained and deeply lined by the outdoor life, with a nose that was too large and dark eyes that were spaced too close together. He was dressed in a cream-coloured suit, the jacket unbuttoned so that the half-breed could see the five-pointed metal star pinned to the left side of his check shirt-front. He wore a gun with fancy butt-plates in a holster which hung low and loose from the right side of his gunbelt. The rig looked as brand new as the white Stetson which he held with both hands by the brim, rotating it slowly in front of his belly.

The half-breed had seen Sheriff Wilde earlier. Along with Stan Barlow, the undertaker, three other men and two women. And had heard, but not listened to, the lawman's questioning of the witnesses. While the women comforted Mrs Donnelly and Barlow oversaw the removal of the body. Now, as he leaned to the side to look beyond the sheriff, he saw that the blonde was back at the table she had left earlier and Warford and his friends were again seated where they had been before the trouble started. Everyone else had left the Red Dog and those who remained were watching Edge intently while they awaited his answer. Outside, the rain was falling steadily: hitting the walls and roof of the saloon hard enough to cover the sounds of the fast-flowing stream.

'Asked you a question, mister,' Wilde said insistently.

'Give a truthful answer and you got nothin' to fear.'

Scorn showed for just part of a second in the half-breed's narrowed eyes as he glanced up at the grim-set face of the lawman. Then he raised his glass and emptied it at a swallow: began to roll a cigarette as he said:

'Warford figured to play some other game but cards. The lady made it plain she wanted no part of it. Bartender warned him off. And got killed for his trouble.'

'It was self-defence, I tell you!' Warford yelled, the tone of his voice and the speed with which he spoke far removed from the manner in which Edge had given his answer to Wilde's question. 'I was just tryin' to be friendly to the lady! Rusty grabbed that damned old scatter-gun of his and I had to—'

'Save it, Dean!' the sheriff flung over his shoulder. 'For the trial. I figure I'm gonna have to arrest you.'

'But I keep—' Warford started again.

And this time was interrupted by Mrs Donnelly who accused bitterly: 'He could have prevented it!' as she emerged from the doorway in back of the bar. Pointed a trembling finger at Edge as he struck a match and lit the freshly-made cigarette. 'A man that can shoot a gun as good as he can, he could've done somethin' to keep it from happenin'.'

She began to sob again, as two women came from the doorway behind her and tried to urge her to return with them into the privacy of the back room.

'Now, now, Estelle,' the sheriff urged. 'It ain't no good any of us talkin' about what might have been. What's done is done and the clocks can't be turned back so it can be done some other way.'

He swung away from Edge and sighed as he went to the table where the four men were seated.

'Wes . . .' Warford started, sober and hungover now: his green eyes pained.

'Gonna have to lock you in a cell, Dean,' Wilde said

ruefully. 'And you ain't gonna give me any trouble, are you? These other boys, they'll ride out to tell Joe Love what happened and he'll do all he can for you.'

'Sure, Dean,' one of Warford's buddies agreed cheerfully. 'You ain't gotta thing to worry about. Mr Love'll have you out quicker than blinkin'.'

'Ain't that the rotten truth,' Estelle Donnelly groaned, exhausted by grief and unable to inject into her voice the depth of contempt that glittered in her flesh-crowded, red-rimmed eyes. 'While my son is bein' eaten by the worms in the ground, his cowardly killer'll have life and freedom bought and paid for with Love greenbacks!'

'No, Estelle, there'll be a fair trial in front of the circuit judge and—'

Wilde curtailed his angry denial, for Mrs Donnelly had swung around and thrust between the two other women to go through the doorway – who glanced with frantic helplessness around the saloon before they went after her.

'All right, Wes,' Dean Warford allowed, obviously feeling easier in his mind now. 'I'll come with you.' He even smiled. 'By the sound of that weather out there, I figure I'm lucky I just have to step around the corner. Instead of riding all the way to the ranch.'

'We'll get right on out there, Dean,' the eldest of the group promised as they all rose to their feet. 'Mr Love'd want that. Wouldn't want you to spend a minute longer than necessary in the gaolhouse.'

'Thanks, boys,' Warford answered, his mood improving by the moment: the good humour shared by his friends.

Which was at odds with that of Wilde, who was still grim-faced while he continued to smart from the fat woman's accusation that in this town, justice went to the highest bidder. Then he sought to off-load some of his ire on the half-breed and the blonde woman when he halted on his way to the batwings in the wake of the quartet of cowpunchers. And looked over his shoulder to share a glare between them as he ordered:

'Necessary for you two people to stay in Irving. To give evidence at the trial.'

'Her especially!' Warford added from the held-open batwings, his voice and face revealing a spiteful anger that was vastly more forceful than Wilde's. 'Hadn't been for her flauntin' her ass in here, there wouldn't have been no trouble!'

'For the trial, Dean,' the sheriff reminded. 'Save it for the proper time.' Then, looking back into the saloon again from the threshold: 'Better have your names. For the record.'

'Dickens,' the woman answered. 'Crystal Dickens.'

The half-breed looked at her rather than the lawman through the smoke coiling from his cigarette as he said: 'Edge. Just Edge.'

And saw her head snap around so that her eyes met his: he impassive and she expressing a degree of surprise that came close to incredulity.

The batwings clattered closed, booted feet stepped down off the stoop, horses were mounted, and parting words were yelled above the beat of hooves on muddy ground.

'You ever been in New York City, mister?' the blonde asked when there was just the falling rain to disturb the stillness.

'Mase never said he was married,' Edge answered. 'And you're too young to have been his mother.'

She rose, picking up the carpetbag and her hat. 'Mason and I were brother and sister. I've been looking for you.'

'Seem to recall I had to keep telling almost everyone in New York that I didn't come from Texas.'

She halted at his table and set the bag down on top of it. 'I came west is all, Mr Edge. It was a crazy thing to do, but I felt I had to attempt it. Trying to find a man in this enormous country. But this does belong to you.'

She reached into the bag and brought out a neatly wrapped-and-tied package. Which she placed beside the bottle and empty glass. The package was about nine inches by six by three.

'It does?' he asked.

'Your blood money. Ten thousand dollars of it.' Then her tone altered from slightly censorious to sourly sarcastic when she added: 'And I hope it buys you a lot of happiness.'

This as she jerked the hat on her head, picked up the bag and swung around to stride toward the doorway, hips swaying and petticoats rustling under the flared skirt of her dress.

Edge poured himself another drink, raised the glass and said: 'I'll drink to that,' as the batwings flapped in the wake of the woman's passing.

And he was in the process of swallowing the whiskey when her face appeared above the tops of the doors and she blurted:

'You don't have to thank me for all the trouble I went to!'

'I didn't,' he answered.

'It costs nothing to say thank you!'

'Talk's cheap, lady,' he countered as he rose from the chair: picked up the bottle with one hand and the package with the other. 'Seems I can afford a lot better than that.'

'I wouldn't touch a cent of that money.'

'Red cent, lady.'

'What?'

'You said it was blood money.'

'And so it is. And if you think I'd lower myself to do

more than pass the time of day with the kind of man you are, you are very much mistaken.'

'It was passing the time of night I was thinking of,' Edge answered and showed a quiet grin along his mouthline as he went toward the doorway. 'And it's not my principles I'm asking you to embrace.'

Three

AN HOUR later, the half-breed lay almost naked under a sheet and blanket on a double bed in a front upper-storey room of the Irving House Hotel: freshly bathed and shaved and with a meal of cold cuts and beans easing comfortingly through his digestive system.

As Sam Pepper had earlier promised, it was a clean bed in a clean room. No frills, unless the net curtain at the window could be classed as such. For the rest there was just the bed, a table beside it, a bureau, a chair and a clothes closet. All standing on a bare floor. No pictures on the walls. A kerosene lamp with a ceramic base on the table.

Crystal Dickens entered the hotel just a few seconds ahead of Edge, but had collected her key, run up the stairs and her room door slammed as he reached the desk at the rear of the spartanly furnished lobby. Where the lanky, sandy-haired, wan-faced Joel Pepper was on duty.

'Your horse is all took care of down at Mr Huber's place, sir,' the boy greeted, a little nervously. 'Pa ain't here right now. But he said to give you room seven. It's a good room and—'

'A single?'

'Yes, sir.'

'Like a double. And a bath. And something to eat.'

'We got a house rule, sir. We don't rent—'

Edge reached a hand into the long hair at the nape of his neck and the Pepper boy broke off with a gasp as he saw the blade of a straight razor jutting from the man's fist. But the half-breed used the razor only to slit open a corner of the paper-wrapped package before he slid it back into the pouch that was held at the nape of his neck by a beaded thong.

'And I got a lot of money, kid. And you got a girl. And just maybe I've got company coming.'

He laid two ten-dollar bills on the desk top.

'I really shouldn't, sir.' He licked his lips and eyed the money eagerly.

'You play organ for the church choir, kid. Figure that'll buy you a place in heaven. But nobody's perfect. Sin a little.'

Joel swallowed hard, reached under the desk and placed down a key. Picked up the money as he urged: 'But I was out back when you came in, mister. You just took a key. By the time I fixed your tub, it was too late to move you out.'

'As a musician, you're a fine liar, kid.'

So now the half-breed relished the comfort of the spacious bed: not smoking or drinking – simply gazing up at the ceiling of the darkened room and listening to the rain falling on the hotel. Thinking about Crystal Dickens.

She was close to thirty. About five six tall and had a figure that looked like it might get overly full-blown if she did not take pains to guard against it. Her darkish blonde hair was worn long and flowed down and over her shoulders in a series of waves. And framed a face that was heart-shaped and not hard to look at in the set of her full lips, pert nose, big brown eyes and dimpled cheeks. Her complexion was a little pale, but it was clear of blemishes: and she knew just how much paint and powder to use to make the most of her natural good looks.

She seemed to be all woman: and from what Edge had seen and heard of her, she was his kind of woman. No ravishing beauty, but even if she had been, his feelings as he lay in the big bed would not have been different. Crystal Dickens struck a chord in him and he had done slightly more than imply an invitation to her. If she accepted, he could hope for a pleasant interlude. And if she did not show up . . . well, the man called Edge never did miss what he had never had. He had lost too much that was his.

Knuckles rapped on the door. And the half-breed reached a bare arm out of the bed and fisted his hand round the frame of the Winchester that lay on the floor.

'It's me,' the blonde called anxiously.

'Key's in the lock,' he answered, releasing his grip on the rifle. 'Use it when you're inside.'

She hesitated for long moments. Then cracked the door open just wide enough so that she could move sideways into the room. There was no lamp on the landing but enough light rose up the stairway from the lobby for Edge to see that she was still fully dressed except for the hat. Then, with the door closed at her back he could see just the pale blur of her face.

The key turned in the lock.

'The Pepper boy told me about you getting a double room,' she said tautly. 'You're not lacking in self-confidence, are you?'

'Comes of being rich.'

She moved away from the door and he heard the floorboards creak under her feet. Then she halted at the side of the bed and said:

'It's the worst kind of rich people who take advantage of the poor. How did you know I was broke?'

Now, as Edge continued to gaze up at the ceiling, he heard the fabric-on-fabric sounds of the woman taking off her clothes.

27

'I didn't.'

She snorted and snapped: 'You simply thought I couldn't resist your many charms?' Then kicked off her boots angrily as she accused: 'You arrogant sonofabitch!'

Edge allowed his breath to expel with the sound of a soft sigh. And murmured as he turned his head on the pillow to look up at her: 'I asked and you came here, lady. What we are and why we do what we do ain't important.'

He could see more than just the paleness of her face in the dark of the room now: for she had stripped herself naked and the entire length and breadth of her body was faintly and alluringly visible in the night. And he experienced an extension of the arousal which had stirred when they looked at each other in the Red Dog after Wilde had asked for their names. But this was gone quicker than it came when she rasped:

'Maybe not to you, mister! But before I get into your bed I want to know how much you'll give me after I leave it!'

'I always pay my way,' he answered, and pulled back the covers for her. The movement was slow and his voice soft. So that what he did next was even more shocking to her because he had revealed not the slightest hint of his intention.

He reached for her with both hands, so fast that she was not aware of it until his left had bunched in her hair at the nape of her neck. And a split second later his right cracked against the flesh of her face. He hit her twice on each cheek. Back handed and with the palm. With an effortless force and speed which left her breathless and unable to move until the brief beating was over. Only then did she feel the smarting pain of the blows: and drew her lips wide to vent a scream as she made to wrench herself away from him.

And found the sound trapped in her throat by the

punishing hand as the one that gripped her hair jerked her closer to the half-breed. She was on her knees on the floor by then, her naked belly folded over the side of the bed and her bared breasts pressed to his forearms. Her stinging face was no more than six inches away from that of her captor.

For no longer than a second he kept his right hand cupped over her mouth and nostrils. Then withdrew it while his left continued to be fisted in her hair. And he spoke as the breath rushed from her lungs and her heartbeat raced.

'I pay my way, but not to have my way, lady,' he said, still softly but with a coldness of tone that she found more terrifying than if he had bellowed at her in a raging temper. 'I don't go with whores.'

Now he jerked her away from him and she gasped at the fresh pain that was triggered at the roots of her hair. He released his hold on her and she came up on her knees, then toppled to the side and sprawled across the floor. Where she whimpered, the sounds trickling from her throat created more by humiliation than the rough treatment she had received.

For many seconds she remained where she was, eyes squeezed tightly closed and huddled up as she tried to control the trembling fit that wracked her naked body. Until Edge said evenly:

'You want some?'

She looked at him and received a tear-and-darkness-hampered impression of him sitting up against the head-board of the bed, extending the bottle of whiskey toward her.

'I . . . I never touch alcohol,' she answered hoarsely.

'You're free, white and over twenty-one,' he told her. 'Make your own decisions.'

He raised the bottle to his own lips and drank from it. Just a swallow.

'I'm not a whore.'

'So no sweat.'

'It's just that down in the saloon . . . you said you could afford more than words . . . and I thought you meant . . .'

She rose unsteadily to her feet, holding the discarded dress modestly in front of her body.

'I meant I'd like to screw you, lady,' he said into the rain-broken silence that followed the trailing off of her disjointed explanation. 'If you wanted to get screwed.' He set the bottle down on the table. 'And the offer still stands. Take it or take off back to your own room.'

He straightened the bedclothes where they had been rumpled by his burst of violence: and left them open.

'You . . . you said just now it wasn't important what we are and why we do things.'

'Exceptions and rules. Guess nothing else got broken.'

'Damn you for a selfish bastard!' she snarled softly, dropped the dress and slid into the bed beside him.

Her face was burning from the blows but her body and limbs were cold against his bed-warmed flesh. He remained in a half-sitting attitude with his shoulders resting on the headboard as she locked her legs around his and embraced him with both arms, pressing her face against the thick growth of hair on his chest.

'You're built as hard as you are,' she whispered after a full minute of silence during which she became as warm as he and ceased to shiver. And moved her fingers across his solidly packed flesh: paused from time to time as her gentle explorations discovered the puckered skin of scar-tissue.

Then her leg moved up his thighs and she uttered a small sound of disappointment: moved a hand down across his belly to double check.

'You said nothing was changed,' she groaned, turning her head to look up at him.

'I ain't the kind that gets a charge out of beating up on a woman,' he told her. And took hold of her by the hair again. Gently this time, to ease her head back down on to his chest. While his other hand flung the bedclothes off before moving to caress her cheek. Then with both hands he applied the lightest of pressure: to ask rather than demand that she slide lower down his body.

'You mean you want . . . you want me to . . . with my mouth . . .' She caught her breath. Then submitted with a sigh to the gentle urging of his hands: and continued to ease downwards when he released her. 'I've never . . . before . . . I don't know if I'll . . . oh, my God, it's starting.'

Her full lips, slightly parted, trailed across the skin of his belly and upper thighs while she whispered the words. And then there was a strange mixture of excitement and awe which triggered a shrillness into her tone as her moving lips found the core of his wanting and drew an immediate response.

'Having a soft spot for a woman is no good at a time like this,' Edge murmured.

'I . . . I . . . I . . .'

'And it's no time, either,' he added, reaching down to cup her cheeks in his hands, 'for a woman to get tongue tied.'

Four

THE FOLLOWING day dawned brightly, the sun glaring down out of a west Texas sky that showed not a trace of the complete cloud-cover that had masked it throughout most of the night. But when Edge opened the window the early-morning air that flowed into the room smelled strongly of the rain-washed land. And he breathed deeply from the freshness of the day which he knew from past experience of countless dawnings in the south-west would not last for long.

While he relished the sensation of the cool, clean air filling his smoke-parched throat and lungs he squinted against the sunlight and surveyed the terrain which spread eastwards from the far bank of the rain-swollen stream. He had seen in the darkness of night that it was hill country, contrasting with the semi-desert flatlands he had ridden across to reach Irving. Now, in the bright sunlight, he was able to see that close to town the slopes and ridges were sandy and rocky, almost barren of vegetation: while further in the east where the hills were higher they were covered with scrubgrass and featured here and there with stands of timber. And far to the north-east, in the direction from which the stream curved to pass the fringe of town, several head of cattle could be seen on a slope.

The cows were the only signs of life out there. And

there were none at all on the street below the hotel window. But people were up and about, if not yet out, in Irving. For the freshness of the damp air was infiltrated with the aromas of woodsmoke, coffee and bacon. Which sparked a new need within Edge as he turned from the window, having satisfied his desire to breathe in the unspoiled newness of early morning. And, he reminded himself when he saw the blanket-covered form of the woman in the bed, after indulging himself in the fulfilment of another of life's pleasures.

Crystal Dickens had been good, he recalled as he stood naked before the bureau, shaving and hardly needing to glance at his reflection in the mirror. Not the best he had ever had – for no woman could surpass the ecstasy he shared so briefly with Beth whose premature and horrifying death had affected him even more deeply than the killing of Jamie. But better than the worst. For this woman had experience enough not to be afraid to learn more: while not being too well grounded to take her partner's wants and responses for granted.

When he was fully dressed, she said: 'That's it, uh?' in a tone of voice, lacking the thickness of sleep, which suggested she had been surreptitiously awake for some time.

'That's what?' he countered as he buckled the gunbelt around his waist.

She moved into a sitting attitude, holding up the blanket around her neck: her face expressing pouting irritation in the frame of her sleep-tousled hair. 'It happened that we both wanted to get laid at the same time. So we did. And now it's over. Unless or until we both want—'

Edge finished tying the holster-lace around his thigh and pulled open a drawer of the bureau. And as he took out the package of money, surprise caused the woman to break off what she was saying. And her big eyes widened

T.O.T. – B

still more as she watched him take some bills from a pants-pocket and push them under the string before he tossed the package on the bed.

'Keep this in mind, lady,' he said flatly. 'Way I see things, there ain't a woman in the world who's worth ten thousand dollars for the rent of her body. For a night or a whole lifetime. So you ain't being paid for sharing my bed.'

He started for the door.

'What on earth . . .?' she began.

'If you only came west to find me and give me that money, you had a wasted trip,' Edge told her. 'It isn't mine.'

'But a man who works for the government told me it was,' the woman came back quickly.

'Lincoln?'

'Yes.'

'He was mistaken. An innocent mistake that put you to a great deal of trouble. On my account. So you keep the money and the account's settled.'

He unlocked the door, opened it and stepped out onto the landing. Crystal Dickens did not say anything until the door was closed again and by that time the half-breed was unable to hear whether she was giving effusive thanks or protesting. For he was already following his nose, which led him down the stairway, across the deserted lobby and under an arch into a small dining-room. Where the bald-headed and paunchy Sam Pepper was seated at a linen-covered table eating a breakfast of ham and eggs and toasted bread.

The hotelman scowled his distaste for the newcomer as he said: 'I told you I didn't want my place used as a whorehouse, mister. Tell you now I won't have my son take money he ain't earned. You got fed last night, had a tub and used the room. You got two square meals to come. One dollar sixty total. When you check out you'll have eighteen forty to come.' He glanced over his shoulder toward a door which stood ajar. 'Joel, one breakfast!'

Edge showed no response to the bitterly spoken words as he moved between other tables, drew out a chair and sat down opposite Pepper. Whose scowl took on a frozen quality and then melted into an expression of sweating fear as he turned from looking at the kitchen doorway and found the muzzle of the half-breed's Frontier Colt hovering an inch away from his nose.

'Is your son a bastard or were you married to his Ma, feller?'

Sam Pepper swallowed hard as his fork rattled on to the plate from his shaking hand. 'She was a decent woman, and a fine wife to me for fifteen years until she died.'

Edge nodded almost imperceptibly. 'And you screwed her lots of times? Not just the once that led to Joel being born?'

Pepper opened his mouth to splutter a protest as his son came in from the kitchen and pulled up short with a sound of horror. And the half-breed continued:

'And you provided for the boy's Ma? Who cooked and cleaned and sewed and nursed you when you were sick and, like I said, shared your bed?'

'Pa, don't rile him!' Joel urged tautly. And looked toward the archway where Crystal Dickens had come to an abrupt halt and was staring at the table where the two men sat.

'That's different,' Sam Pepper squeezed out from his fear constricted throat. And licked beads of sweat off his top lip.

'Sure it is,' Edge agreed evenly. 'It's just a matter of what a woman is prepared to sell herself for. But there's a line between women of certain kinds. And it ain't drawn by a preacher at an altar.'

'Edge, stop this!' the hurriedly dressed blonde in the archway pleaded.

'Pepper called you a whore,' the half-breed answered as a sound of nails being hammered into timber rang out from the street. 'Just telling him what side of the line you got laid on!'

'Oh my God!' she squealed, her pale face shading to deep red. Then whirled around and hurried across the lobby to jerk open a door and carry her shame and embarrassment outside.

'Going to put the gun away now, feller,' Edge said, and matched his action with the words. 'But if you insult Miss Dickens again that way, it won't be you who sends for the lawman and the mortician. Right, kid. I'm ready to eat.'

Pepper took out a handkerchief and frantically mopped sweat beads off his face: as his son came tentatively to the table, looking anxiously at him. Then the boy set down the laden plate and coffee cup with an angry heavy-handedness as he raked his eyes from his father, to the deserted archway and at Edge.

'You got a strange way of goin' about things, mister,' he said tautly.

'How's that, kid.'

'If you think so highly of that lady you didn't oughta talk dirty about her the way you did. In front of her and all.'

'Forget it, Joel,' his father advised grimly.

'I don't think anything of the lady, kid,' Edge said. 'It wasn't her reputation your Pa was muddying up.'

He began to eat, while the father and son stared at him incredulously. Then acknowledged that they believed him by expressing disgust. This as the hammering sounds from the street were curtailed. Then Sam Pepper pushed back his chair and rose, leaving his breakfast only half eaten.

'We can rely on you checkin' out today, mister?' he asked coldly.

'It's your place, feller. And you're entitled to make the rules. No sweat.'

'You have to stay in town for the trial,' Pepper said with less animosity: seemed surprised at the easiness of the half-breed's attitude. 'Don't reckon Estelle will open the Red Dog after what's happened. But there's some families in Irving that take boarders.'

'Obliged.'

They left him to his breakfast, Joel carrying the dirty dishes into the kitchen and his father stepping through into the lobby and then going out onto the street. Edge ate slowly and when he was finished he rolled and smoked the first cigarette of the day, conscious of the rising heat. And a few moments after he swallowed the last of his coffee he smelled the smoke of strong tobacco which was carried by the hot air entering the hotel through the open doorway.

He went up to his room and as he collected his gear, heard hoofbeats in the distance: glanced from the window and saw a group of riders far out on the east trail. Approaching town without haste.

Down in the lobby, Sam Pepper was waiting for him in the doorway, smoking a strong-smelling cheroot.

'Your change, mister,' he said, thrusting some bills and coins at Edge. 'And it seems the Red Dog could be openin' today after all. Under new management.'

The half-breed accepted the money with a nod and pushed it into a pocket of his pants. Then stepped out onto the stoop which at this time in the morning provided no shade from the glaring sun. He glanced to his left and saw the reason for the recent hammering sounds. A length of timber had been nailed to a stoop-support out front of the saloon, its painted lettering still wet and running. It proclaimed simply: FOR SALE.

Still holding his saddle and bedroll under one arm, Edge pointed with his free hand to where the approaching riders were visible through the trees on the stream bank. 'Be Warford's boss coming to spring him from the gaolhouse, I guess?'

'Joe Love and some of his hands from the Howlin' Coyote spread sure enough,' Pepper answered as he advanced across the threshold. 'Known all over the state for the way he takes care of his men. Don't like trouble. Had more than his fair share of that while he was buildin' up his place.'

'We all have our dislikes, feller,' Edge said, and directed a spit out onto the street which was already becoming dusty under the drying rays of the sun. 'One of mine is staying in the same place too long. You know when the circuit judge will be in town?'

'Wes Wilde telegraphed San Antone last night. The judge oughta be on the noon stage tomorrow.'

'Obliged,' the half-breed muttered and moved along the stoop, stepped down off the end and then up onto that fronting the saloon. This as the batwings swung open and Crystal Dickens and Estelle Donnelly emerged: the older and much heavier woman attired in deep mourning, complete with an all-concealing veil hanging down across her face.

'This place open to rent rooms?' he asked.

'That ain't up to—' Mrs Donnelly started.

'It's been sold, Mr Edge,' Crystal cut in as the horses of the group from the ranch beat upon the planking of the bridge. 'I'm just taking her over to the land office to attend to the papers.'

Then she gripped the fat woman's upper arm and they both turned their backs to the half-breed: halted when the riders reined in their mounts and a man called:

'Estelle!'

Edge looked at the group. There were six men astride

horses in the settling dust. The three who had been playing cards with Dean Warford in the saloon last night. Two others, in their mid-twenties, who were dressed in the same workaday cowpuncher's garb. And a tall, thin, grey-haired man of about sixty attired in a dark blue city suit, white lace-trimmed shirt, black bootlace tie, black-and-white riding boots and a white ten-gallon hat. He removed the hat when the two women turned to look at him, and out of the shade of its brim his face was seen to be handsomely distinguished, with a great deal of character stained and lined into the skin.

'I was mighty sorry to hear about Rusty gettin' killed, Estelle,' he offered, and abandoned his mournful expression for a moment to scowl at his men. Who responded by removing their own hats. 'He was a fine man and a good son to his Ma. It's a terrible thing, him gettin' gunned down in such a foolish manner.'

'My son was murdered, Joe Love,' Mrs Donnelly answered coldly from behind her veil. 'Shot like a dog by that no-account, no-good coward Warford!'

Hardness glittered in the tall rancher's green eyes, but for the most part his expression matched his morose tone when he countered: 'Now, now, Estelle. I can understand you being bitter. But let's not pre-judge this thing until justice has been seen to be done.'

Crystal made to move the woman along the stoop, but she wrenched free of the hold on her arm and whirled to snarl at Love: 'That won't never happen in this town with one of your hands on the receivin' end, Joe Love! And I don't intend to stay around and see nothin'. My son's dead and our place has been sold. I'm gonna sign the papers, see Rusty go to his final restin' place and then ride the eastbound stage outta Irving. That's what I'm gonna do!'

She swung around again and set off along the stoop. Crystal was taken by surprise and had to hurry in her wake: did not catch up with her until the older woman started to turn the corner onto Lone Star Street.

'The woman with Mrs Donnelly is the one the trouble was about, Mr Love. And that there feller is the one we told you about.'

Love looked from the man who spoke to Edge as all of them put their hats back on their heads. Said:

'Mornin' to you, stranger. Only natural the lady is a little overwrought. Just tell the truth about what you saw last night and you got no worries.'

'Been a long time since I worried about anything, feller,' the half-breed answered.

Love surveyed him for just a second or so longer, then nodded as if he had reached a decision. And sighed as he shifted his steady gaze to Pepper.

'Hell of a thing, Sam,' he said ruefully. 'Times I've told that young hot-head to count up to ten before doin' anythin' when he's riled.'

'Keep your own advice in mind, Joe,' the hotelman advised. 'If the kid's guilty, he's guilty.'

Anger paid a brief visit to the rancher's hat-shaded face. And was seen again in the abrupt way he jerked on the reins and used his spurs to turn and move his horse forward. Was heard in his sarcastic tone of voice when he growled:

'Point taken, Mr Mayor.'

Pepper grimaced in the wake of the riders, snatched the butt of the cheroot from his lips and hurled it angrily out into the dust stirred up by the hooves.

'Feller that likes to have his own way, I figure,' Edge said.

'Makes two of you!' Pepper snarled and whirled to enter his hotel.

The half-breed moved more slowly into the saloon, which still smelled faintly of liquor, tobacco smoke, sweat and exploded black powder from the night before.

And had to move halfway into the long room to find a table beyond the glaring sunlight which entered through the doorway and flanking windows. Where he sat and waited, listening to the flowing stream and needing to make a conscious effort to keep his mind from futile thoughts about the immediate future. Did this by recalling memories of that part of his past from which Crystal Dickens had sprung.

It had been a bad time in New York City. In terms of the violence that erupted around him, no worse than a lot of other times, maybe: but because he was out of his element in a landscape featured with towering buildings, traffic-choked streets and throngs of people instead of mountains and deserts and small towns like Irving, it seemed in retrospect like some kind of waking nightmare.

Just one good thing had emerged from his run-in with the crime bosses and their gangs who were fighting to control the city's underworld. A pardon from Washington on a murder he had committed many years before in Kansas – when he was Josiah C. Hedges on the trail of the ex-troopers who killed Jamie. The only killing for which the law had posted wanted-flyers on him.

A government agent named Lincoln had offered him the amnesty as a reward for acting as the catalyst in the struggle between the opposing criminal factions. And this had been enough for him. He did not want the ten thousand dollars which one of the crime bosses had offered him – did more than offer. Paid into the bank account of a newspaper reporter named Mason Dickens who had tagged onto the half-breed in search of a story.

A woman's footfalls clicking on the boarding of the stoop interrupted Edge's train of thought and he looked up as Crystal Dickens turned into the saloon doorway and halted, in silhouette against the bright morning sunlight.

'Fifty-fifty,' she announced.

'What's that, lady?'

She came into the Red Dog and weaved between the intervening tables, petticoats rustling as they had the previous night. When she was in the shaded area, halted before the table where he sat, he could see her face in detail: the satisfied expression which was set firmly on her features. She was holding a folded piece of stiff, legal paper which she let fall on to the table.

'Mrs Donnelly accepted the offer I made for title of this place, Mr Edge. Five thousand dollars for all of it: lock, stock and barrel. That's the bill of sale. Made out in your name.'

'I sometimes drink in saloons, lady,' the half-breed said evenly. 'At running one I don't—'

'Shut up for awhile and listen!' she cut in on him. And drew out a chair and sat down opposite him. Now she expressed determination. 'Mason and me weren't close after he left our home in New England to go to New York. I used to make excuses for it in the old days. But then I came to realise it was because I was jealous of him. Going to the big city and doing what he wanted to do while I had to stay home and tend our mother. Who was always sick and got sicker after Mason left. Then Mason got killed and when she heard about it, it meant the end for mother.

'Six weeks it took for her broken heart to finally stop. And then it was my chance to go to the city. But it didn't turn out like I expected. Rotten jobs, stinking places to live in and rotten stinking men.'

'Figured you didn't do your training in some little Vermont town,' Edge said.

She snorted. 'Vermont folks are the same as Irving folks and New York folks,' she rasped. 'Way mother was, I didn't get much of a chance to meet people in my home town. Here there hasn't been the time. In New York, I just picked the wrong ones.' She shook her head, her blonde hair catching stray beams of sunlight. 'But I didn't come here to talk about that, Mr Edge. In New York I finally got around to straightening out Mason's affairs. And I thought I'd struck a pot of gold when I found out he had ten thousand dollars plus interest in a bank. But after I got over being excited about it, I started to worry about how he came by so much. And I asked some questions.

'Which led me to this man Lincoln. And he told me all about how and why Mason was killed and who was involved. You played a large part in what he told me, Mr Edge. How it was Mason fastened onto you and not the other way around. And about the money being yours.

'I'd had enough of New York by then. And there was nothing for me to go back home for. So I decided to come out west and look for you.'

'Like you said last night, crazy,' he growled as he dug out the makings and started to roll a cigarette.

She shook her head. 'Not so crazy, mister. As I told you, the money in the bank made interest. And I planned to keep looking for as long as the interest allowed. Then if I hadn't found you, I planned to use the money as if it were my own.'

Edge lit the cigarette and used the dead match to push the bill of sale a few inches toward her. 'Like I said lady, Lincoln was mistaken. The money belonged to a man named Boss Black. He wanted me to do a job for him and I wanted no part of it. Way it turned out, I killed—'

'I said for you to shut up and—'

'I've heard enough,' he told her, his level tone at odds with her shrill anger. 'You came out west on a bum steer. If having the money gives you a conscience, go back east and track down the heirs of Boss Black. They're the ones the money rightfully belongs to.'

She stood up so sharply her chair rocked back and leaned against one at a nearby table. 'Like hell I will, mister!' she snarled. 'I've been on the move for more than six months, riding trains and stages from one hick town to another. Asking in saloons, ballrooms, railroad depots, way stations, ranches and some other places if anyone had heard of you. And it hasn't been easy, mister! More times than not, men like that Warford kid gave me hard times. And I'm not about to go through anything like that again. I've found you and now you tell me it was all for nothing. Well, I'm not prepared to accept that, mister.

'I did what I did in good faith. In another few weeks the interest would have run out and I would have got to keep the whole ten thousand. Without any pangs of conscience. But coincidence caused us to meet up last night. And I was ready to give you what I honestly believed to be your just dues.

'You didn't want it. Which I find real hard to understand of a man like you. But all right. You'll sure as hell have half of it, one way or another. Call it half the finder's fee. Call it what the hell you like. Burn this place down or ride off and leave it for squatters to come in and take over. As far as I'm concerned, I've paid you for a favour you did the family. According to Mr Lincoln. And I don't think he was mistaken about how you looked out for Mason. Good day, Mr Edge.'

She flounced out of the saloon, then did an about turn to re-appear in the doorway and add quickly:

'I don't go to the bed of any man who crooks his finger at me, mister! I came to yours because you and Mason were friends! We weren't close but he was my brother and you looked out for him when he needed someone to do that! And I didn't want money for the use of my body! I figured I deserved payment for the trouble I took! But not that much! I'm happy with half!'

'Why be?' he asked evenly. 'You're better than half the woman I thought you were when I first saw you.'

'What you think doesn't matter to me,' she answered. 'My conscience is clear.'

'Enjoy the money, lady.'

'I intend to, mister.'

'And you know where to find me.'

'Why on earth should I want to do that?'

He smiled at her silhouetted form in the doorway. 'In case your conscience – or anything else – wants a little prick.'

Five

THE MAN called Edge did not usually drink hard liquor before midday, but this morning he made an exception. Took the half-finished bottle of whiskey from a saddle-bag and went behind the bar counter to get a shot glass. He poured a slug from the bottle, looked down at it for a moment, raised it in the manner of a toast as he raked his eyes around the saloon, then threw the rye against the back of his throat.

There had been the farmstead in Iowa which he and Jamie had inherited jointly from their parents. And the small shack and piece of land in the Dakotas which he had purchased when he married Beth. Now for the third time in his life he had title to something he could not ride, wear or use to kill people. And after so many years of being free of such an encumbrance, his new situation would take some coming to terms with.

But morning-drinking would not help him do this, he decided, and he recorked the bottle. Left it and the glass on the bartop and went to survey the extent of what he owned. Owned, anyway, according to the bill of sale the woman gave him. But if he chose to stick to his principles concerning the true ownership of the money, then the Red Dog saloon with its mean living-quarters at the rear and the six crudely furnished rooms for rent on the upper floor did not belong to him. And Crystal Dickens had suggested two of many courses he could take if he felt so strongly about accepting this undeserved reward.

Then, as he opened the rear door and surveyed the garbage-littered back lot of the building, he growled: 'What the hell.'

And a man countered: 'I ain't trespassin', mister. I used to work here. You the new owner? You still want me?'

He emerged from a derelict out-building which bordered the south side of the saloon's back lot, dividing it from that of the hotel. A Negro in his sixties, short and skinny with sharp features and sad eyes. With a half-circle of grey hair around the back of his skull and a heavy covering of bristles on his lower face. Dressed in much patched denim pants and a ragged shirt. Carrying a battered hat in one hand and a shovel in the other. He looked frightened.

'As it happens, I wasn't meaning you, feller,' Edge told him. 'Thinking aloud.'

The Negro showed his relief with an eager smile. 'Name's Moses, mister. Like the baby in the rushes in the Bible. I done the cleanin' and heavy liftin' and the fixin' up of what went wrong for Mr Donnelly and his Ma. Dollar a day is what I was paid, and allowed to sleep in this old stable. If you want me to keep on doin' like I used to, I will, mister. I did the cleanin' up this mornin'. And I painted and fixed the for sale sign.'

'You ever serve drinks, feller?'

A vigorous shake of the head. 'No, sir. Can tell you're a stranger in this part of the country. Folks around here, they wouldn't take kindly to no black man pourin' their liquor and handlin' the glasses they drank outta.'

'Then those that think that way will have to go thirsty, Moses,' Edge told him. 'I'll pay two dollars a day and you'll tend bar as well as everything else.'

The increase in pay excited the black man, but his mood was soured by anxiety. 'I'm real glad you asked me, mister. But if nobody comes here to drink, how you gonna make the place pay?'

'Just do the job, feller. But don't count on it lasting too long. First thing I want is for you to take down the for sale notice. Then paint out the Red Dog sign.'

'You gonna give the place a new name, mister?'

Edge took out a dime, tossed it and glanced down at where it fell in the dust. 'Heads. Paint up The Lucky Break, feller.'

'What would it have been if the coin came down tails, mister?'

'The Unlucky Break,' the half-breed answered as he made to turn back into the kitchen of the saloon.

'Mister? I'd like to do somethin' else before I start in for you?'

'You can wash up and shave,' Edge told him and dug out some crumpled bills from the change Sam Pepper had given him. A five and five ones, which he screwed into a ball and tossed toward the Negro, who caught the money in his hat. 'And go to the store and buy some decent clothes, uh?'

'That's a lot of days' work, mister,' the Negro said morosely after glancing into his hat.

'House uniform,' Edge told him. 'The house buys it.'

Suddenly the black man's eyes looked so sad that he seemed to be on the point of tears. 'Mister, ain't no one ever—'

'Just make sure you don't cry in other people's beer, feller.'

'It kinda makes it hard for me to ask what I was gonna.'

'Ask.'

'Mr Donnelly and his Ma, they was pretty good to me. None better in this town. I reckoned I'd go dig the grave for him.'

'Local folks won't mind you doing that?'

Moses showed a bitterly sardonic grin. 'Lotsa folks think that diggin's all a spade's fit for, mister.'

Edge matched the other man's expression as he drawled: 'Figure it'll come as a real shock to them when they find out this saloon ain't got a colour bar.'

He heard Moses chuckling as the black man went around the end of the falling-down stable toward the cemetery out back of the chapel. And he went through the kitchen and parlour to the saloon. Which was as empty of customers as when he had left it. But something had changed – on the bartop beside the whiskey bottle and glass was Crystal Dickens' carpetbag.

He crossed to the batwings and pushed through them to step out onto the stoop. Smelled burning tobacco and glanced to his right: saw Sam Pepper in the doorway of the hotel, smoking another cheroot.

'The lady was lookin' for you,' the hotel owner and mayor of Irving reported flatly. 'It was her choice to check out of my place. I told her about the folks that take in boarders.'

There was a brand of embarrassed regret in the fat man's tone and attitude – as if he felt the need to apologise but could not bring himself to speak the words.

'I'm not lost, feller,' the half-breed answered, and muttered for his own ears as he turned and started toward the corner: 'Just temporarily misplaced.'

The lack of noise and movement on White Creek Road – the name painted on the saloon façade up under the eaves – was in contrast with the activity on Lone Star Street. Where women with baskets moved from store to store or stood in pairs and groups talking, men carried bales and sacks and crates from doorways to wagons, the blacksmith was shoeing a horse out front of the open doors of his forge, small children played shrill games while older ones recited their times tables in the schoolhouse, a patent-medicine salesman was holding the attention of a small gathering at the rear of his wagon and a half-dozen Mexicans were engaged in restoration work on the mission church.

There were more people on the street and in the business premises than lived in Irving. Farmers and their wives, he guessed, who had not entered town from the east trail. Then, as he drew level with the mission, he saw that another trail entered Irving at the side of the church: from the low, rolling hill-country to the north.

As he strolled along the south side of the street in the hot shade of the boardwalk awning, the half-breed sensed an underlying atmosphere of tension that had not been immediately apparent when he turned the corner and got a first impression of the slow-paced activity on the street.

Those people who greeted him did so absently, then did a double-take. While many more appeared not to notice him until he was past, when he became aware of the surreptitious glances they shot at him. But, he quickly came to realise, he was of relatively minor interest to the citizens of Irving and the out-of-towners. Who, in doing whatever business or chores engaged them in the commercial centre of Irving, felt drawn to look often toward the façade of the sheriff's office: where six horses were hitched to the rail.

The brick-built lawman's office was on the north side of the street, beyond the mission church and the end of the north trail, between an adobe building which housed a dry-goods store and the frame-fronted premises of the Huber Livery Stables. It was toward this last that the half-breed was headed when he stepped down off the sidewalk and angled across the street. And sensed animosity directed toward him from behind the sun-glinting windows of the law office. But the one-piece wooden door remained firmly closed and it was almost possible to feel against his skin the relief that was generated by the people on the street as he entered the hot, horse-smelling shade of the livery.

'Reckon you're Edge,' a man growled unhappily from a stall.

'You've got the name right. You also know what everyone else in this town does about me?'

'What's that, Mr Edge?'

He emerged from the stall with a pail in his hand. A man of fifty or so. Not tall, but broadly built, with muscular flesh rather than fat pressing against the fabric of his shirt and pants. Curly-headed and with a round, florid face featured with small dark eyes, a snub nose and a small mouth. A dull-looking man who, if he did lack brains, made up for it with brawn.

'I wouldn't know, feller. But whatever it is it seems to scare them.'

He looked into the stall and saw that a foal only a few days old was lying on the straw inside, nose white from the milk-feed Huber had given her.

'Orphan?'

'Yeah. You're the new owner of the Red Dog? Word is from the land office.'

'Yeah.'

'Saw one of Love's hands gun down Rusty Donnelly last night?'

'Right.'

'And plan on tellin' the court it wasn't self-defence?'

'Why should that scare anyone but the Warford kid?'

'He's like the foal, Mr Edge. He's an orphan.'

'Me, too,' the half-breed answered and went to the stall where his gelding had spent the night.

'And me. But we didn't get kinda adopted by Joe Love.'

Gently, Edge backed his horse out of the stall which was clean and had some feed still in the box. 'You give a good service for fifty cents, feller,' he said.

'The preacher don't charge a thing for his services,' Huber countered flatly. 'Any kind.'

'How does he make a living?'

'Love endows the chapel. You're takin' the geldin' out because there's a stable at the Red Dog, I guess?'

'Right.' Edge dug some coins from a pants pocket and placed four bits on the table where Huber had set down the pail.

'This is a small town. Part of a close-knit community. There's a certain order of things around here. Ain't everyone agrees with it, but they abides by the rules because, on the whole, it's a pretty good place to live in.'

'Ain't just foaling mares that die in it, feller,' the half-breed said evenly as he led the gelding by the reins toward the open doorway.

'Reckon I've talked around what I had to say, Mr Edge,' Huber growled. 'But you got my meanin', I guess?'

'Figure others will try to make it plainer?' Edge said, looking back over his shoulder at the liveryman.

Huber smiled wanly. 'Felt I had to offer a friendly warnin'. I'm one of them that don't agree with the way some things are. Luck to you.'

Edge spat at the hard-packed, hoof-trampled floor of the livery. 'Tell you something about luck, Huber,' he growled. 'The harder people work at whatever they want, the luckier they get at it.'

The grin froze on the florid face and the man snarled: 'Talk's easy, stranger. But the storm you'll maybe talk up could give you a real hard time!'

'Obliged for your concern, feller.'

'And not just for you!' Huber called after him as he led the gelding out on to the sun-bright street. At the same time as Love and his men emerged from the law office: the group made up of seven now for Warford was with them. Then, a few moments later, four sombrely-clad pallbearers came out of Barlow's Funeral Parlour which was directly across the street from the livery stable.

The quartet carried a plain pine coffin which they eased carefully into the glass-sided hearse parked by the sidewalk, under the anxious supervision of the frock-coated and top-hatted Stan Barlow who Edge recognised from his visit to the saloon the previous night. When the casket was safely inside, the rear door of the hearse was closed and fastened. And then a young preacher with a surplice over his cassock came out of the funeral parlour, followed by Estelle Donnelly and Crystal Dickens, the younger woman supporting the arm of the elder.

The town had become silent and remained so while the elderly mortician moved around the hearse to take hold of the bridle of one of the pair of black-plumed horses: and the preacher, two mourners and four pall-bearers took their places behind the vehicle. The scrape of bootleather on dusty street sounded very loud: then was masked by the turning of wheels and slow beat of hooves as the cortège moved off.

Without exception, every male bystander removed his hat. Women bowed their heads as the funeral procession rolled and shuffled by.

'It could've been me in there, Mr Love,' Dean Warford growled.

'Shut your stupid mouth, you hot-headed sonofa-bitch!' the rancher rasped venomously. 'And pay your respects!'

'I ask no respects from—' the bereaved mother started.

'Please, ma'am,' the young preacher hissed. 'Let us not sully this most solemn of occasions.'

The funeral had progressed beyond the mission church before Joe Love signalled to his men – by donning his big hat – that they were at liberty to move and speak. This as, yard by yard, the town's business activity was resumed after the passing of the hearse.

'Mount up, men,' the distinguished-looking rancher ordered. Then looked hard-eyed at Edge when he was astride his own horse. 'Understand you've purchased the Red Dog, sir.'

'Would seem so, feller.'

'I wish you a long and prosperous stay in our town. And there's no reason why that shouldn't be so. Last night's unfortunate incident was not representative of Irving, sir. Trouble of any kind is very much a stranger here.'

'Just like you,' Warford rasped at the half-breed.

Just as earlier, the people on the street were devoting only part of their attention to their chores: but now they cast furtive glances in just one direction.

'It was a mistake,' Love went on. 'A terrible and tragic mistake. Which the young are prone to make from time to time.'

'Nobody's perfect,' Edge drawled.

'Quite so, sir. But we do the best we can. The people of this community of ours consider themselves extremely fortunate to live in what they think of as God's own place in God's own country. But when we make human mistakes we ensure that justice is always tempered with mercy. As I am sure it will be in this instance. Good day to you.'

He backed his horse away from the rail and tugged on the reins to turn him. His men followed his example, but then aped Dean Warford in the way they shot menacing glances back over their shoulders at the half-breed.

The town's lawman stepped onto the threshold of his office as Edge watched the group of cattlemen ride away down the street, Love responding with a touch of his hat brim to the many greetings that were directed to him.

'It's a hell of a long way from being heaven on earth,

mister,' Wilde said. 'But I'd say you weren't no angel. So why start a fire that could burn some people who don't deserve it?'

'Told him more or less the same thing, Wes,' Jake Huber muttered from the doorway of his livery.

The two Irving men eyed each other, a little shame-faced.

'Maybe that good old boy is right,' Edge said pensively.

'Glad you see it that way,' the sheriff said with a sigh that was at odds with his spoken sentiments.

'Maybe this really is God's own place,' the half-breed went on, and spat into the dust out of the side of his mouth as he urged the gelding forward. 'But if it is, I don't figure God is Love.'

Six

EDGE sensed relief in the hot morning air as he led the gelding along the busy main street of Irving: where the tempo of daily life had quickened. There was a great deal of happy laughter in the talk, people seemed to move with a new-found lightness in their tread, there were easy smiles for the half-breed as he passed, and friendly warmth in the greetings spoken to him. No more did the men and women constantly interrupt their mundane domestic and business assignments to direct secret attention toward a centre of potential trouble.

The atmosphere, he thought, was probably much as it would have been had the people watched a Texas twister whirling toward them – then seen it make a sudden deviation and race away to spare their town from its path of destruction. They had been terribly frightened, but now the threat was removed.

Save for a few exceptions here and there among the throng of people – men and some women who turned their heads away from the cool and level gaze of Edge's ice-blue eyes, to hide from him the same brand of shame which he had seen in the faces of Jake Huber and Sheriff Wes Wilde.

Then he turned the corner onto the deserted stretch of White Creek Road, having put the town and its problems out of his mind. Until he stood for a few moments to survey the weathered frame façade of the saloon: while Joel Pepper played soft and mournful organ music badly and the young preacher intoned the graveside funeral service. Then he experienced a stab of cold anger in the pit of his stomach. Which expanded when the music and prayer ended and he heard a distant thunder of galloping hoofbeats, turned and looked through the streamside trees to glimpse the rancher and his men just before they rode out of sight beyond a rise.

'It's the law hereabouts, mister,' Sam Pepper said from the doorway of the hotel. 'Long as cash-money is posted with the sheriff, a prisoner waitin' to be tried gets bailed out. Town council meetin' last night set bail on Dean Warford at a thousand dollars.'

'I care, feller?'

'You look like you care about somethin', that's for sure.'

'Just me,' Edge told him and led his horse along the alley between the saloon and the hotel. Then thought, but did not say aloud: . . . *and what's mine*. For, aside from the basic question of whether he was morally entitled to ownership of the Red Dog, he was not certain whether he wanted the place. Knew only that if he did, he wanted no part of the kind of town where the people walked in dread of an uncrowned ruler. But short of dismantling the saloon and shipping it elsewhere to be rebuilt . . .

'Okay, mister, I'm ready to go to work for you,' Moses announced as he entered the stable where Edge was installing the horse. 'I dug a fine grave for Mr Donnelly so somebody else can fill it in. I'll get right on with the new sign paintin' and then I'll go buy my new clothes.'

The black man's sharp-featured face slipped easily out of its mournful set to show a grin of pleasure.

'Like for you to have some feed sent over for my horse, feller. And bring in some drinking water.'

'I'll sure do that, mister. But can I move the animal to another stall? He's in the one where I sleep.'

Edge glanced up at the sagging roof and then at the holed walls of the delapidated building. 'Figured you picked the warmest and driest place, Moses. From now on you sleep inside the saloon.'

The negro looked anxious.

'Something wrong?'

He sighed. 'Just hope you know what you're doin', mister. You already made sure you won't get no drinkin' customers. Havin' me tend the bar. And with me beddin' down in one of the rooms, you sure as hell won't get nobody rentin' the rest of them.'

Edge showed a bitter grin: 'Really am blackening my character around here, ain't I?'

Again he heard the Negro chuckling as he left him to go into the Red Dog, the bar-room of which was still deserted. But it was a little cooler in there now that the sun had climbed high enough up the eastern dome of the cloudless sky so that its glare fell short of the doorway and flanking windows.

He waited until the hearse and the people involved in the interment of Rusty Donnelly had moved back along White Creek Road and turned into Lone Star Street before he took a chair out onto the shaded stoop and sat down: to roll, light and smoke a cigarette. Then he sank lower in the chair and tipped his hat forward so that its brim masked the pleasant view of timber, flowing stream and low hill-country beyond. He did not doze, speculate on the future or reflect on the past. Merely enjoyed the peace and solitude. And did not have to make any effort to keep from his mind images of hatred and revulsion he had seen on certain faces as people returning from the funeral glanced into the saloon.

After awhile, he heard Moses climb out of a front upper-storey window. Then smelled paint. The Negro began to whistle happily as he worked on the sign. Footfalls hit the boarding of the hotel stoop, then moved along the street. They halted and there was the sound of nails being wrenched from timber. Edge tipped his hat back on the top of his head and saw Sam Pepper, an angry, tight-lipped frown on his fleshy face, in process of tearing down the for sale sign.

'Got a feller working for me who was going to do that,' the half-breed said evenly.

Pepper tossed the sign on to the stoop. 'Word is you've hired on that nigger to do more than the shit chores, mister!' Pepper rasped. 'So best you keep that sign handy. On account of you'll need it again when you go broke from havin' no customers.'

Moses had curtailed his whistling.

'You going downtown, feller?' Edge asked.

'I am. Stage is due and I'm expectin' guests to be aboard.'

'Word spreads fast in this town, uh?'

'What you gettin' at, mister?' His anger was undermined by perplexity now.

'About me having title to this place and about the help I've hired. Guess everyone knows who and what he is. Moses, who's a Negro. Or a black. Like for you to make it known that if I hear anyone call him nigger I'll treat them the same way as if they'd called me a greaser.'

'You make your own threats, mister!' Pepper snarled as he turned and strode away.

'Just did,' Edge called after him.

'Man, oh man,' Moses rasped softly from up on the stoop awning. 'You sure are fixin' to make things hard for yourself in this town, mister.'

'It's where I'm living for awhile, feller,' the half-breed answered as he tipped his hat over his eyes again. 'And where a man lives he ought to feel at home.'

Thirty minutes later, after the Negro had finished the

sign and gone for the horse-feed and his new clothes, Sam Pepper came back along White Creek Road, obsequiously accompanying two middle-aged couples and an elderly woman who looked uncomfortably hot and dishevelled in their smart city-clothes after a gruelling stage-ride.

'Morning,' Edge offered as he raised his hat from his eyes, touched the brim but did not alter his relaxed posture in the chair.

The two men averted their heads and the three women made ladylike sounds of disgruntlement. Sam Pepper showed a self-satisfied smirk as he ushered his guests over the final few yards to the hotel entrance.

'Never did say it was a good one,' the half-breed murmured.

Then stared fixedly out across the street, through the foliage of the trees, over the stream and at a point on a distant hill-crest. For a stretched second he saw just a patch of brown brush. But then again something shiny flashed in the sunlight. Just a pinpoint of glitter against the gently-rolling terrain. Almost a mile away and half that distance north of the trail. It could have been caused by a hundred and one innocent things. But the puff of white smoke was unmistakable.

With a grunt of anger, Edge powered himself forward from the chair: and threw himself to the side the instant he was clear of its arms. His ears were attuned to catch the crack of the gunshot and he heard it as his shoulder hit the stoop boarding. But nobody else could have separated it from the noise made by the stage as it came around the corner with four fresh and eager horses in the traces. He heard also, almost in unison with the report, the thud of the bullet burying itself in the timber of the saloon wall: looked up and saw wood splinters fly from a point six inches above the top strut of the bow-back chair in which he had been seated.

'Is the man mad?' one of the women on the hotel stoop exclaimed.

'I think he's having a fit,' another countered.

The stage rolled by amid whirling dust and he glimpsed Estelle Donnelly's face at a window. In profile, the veil removed, set in an expression of grim determination. Then the Concord was gone by, swinging into the turn to rumble and rattle over the bridge. And Edge was on his feet, in the saloon doorway and poised to hurl himself against the batwings if he saw the tell-tale puff of muzzle-smoke to signal another shot.

'Making too free with his stock-in-trade looks like,' one of Pepper's newly arrived male guests said haughtily. 'Falling down drunk.'

The whole group went into the lobby of the Irving House. This as, up on the crest of the distant hill, the sharpshooter with the high-velocity rifle fitted with a telescopic sight stood up from the brush, turned and ran down the far slope of the rise. And Moses came around the corner, lean body clothed in a grey suit, balancing a loosely packed sack on his shoulder with his head craned to the side so that his black derby would not be dislodged.

'Well, mister,' he announced happily. 'Folks don't object to takin' your money. All we gotta do now is wait and see if they'll come here and spend what they got with you.'

Edge ignored him to take a closer look at the bullet imbedded in the wall, at a point where his head would have been in the way had he not hurled himself out of the chair.

'Somethin' botherin' you, mister?' the Negro asked, his joy abruptly ended.

'Something, feller. But better to have something on my mind than a bullet in my brain.' He turned and gestured with a hand to the country beyond the stream.

'How far over there is the boundary line of the Howling Coyote range?'

'Creek is it.'

'Just the Love hands out there then?'

'Except on the trail. That's a public right of way.' Moses stopped alongside Edge and whistled. 'Hey, ain't that a bullet hole, mister?'

'No sweat,' Edge said evenly. 'At least I know who to sue for the damage.'

The Negro swallowed hard. 'Guess I'll go tend to your animal's needs, mister,' he said, and scuttled hurriedly into the saloon.

The half-breed followed at a more leisurely pace, after a final survey of the Howling Coyote's western section: on which nothing was moving except the grazing cattle to the north and the stage along the trail. He moved behind the bar, one hand fisting around the bottle and the other the glass. But did not pour himself a drink before the hands on the clock fixed to the rear wall came together to mark midday.

This as whispering voices and footfalls sounded out on the street. But he had time to sit at the table where his gear rested before the batwings opened and Crystal Dickens entered: trailed by a bunch of men, most of whom Edge recognised from his visit to Lone Star Street earlier.

'I moved out of the hotel, Mr Edge,' the blonde woman said. 'Like to stay here if I may?'

'Sure. Nice of you to bring your friends.'

'These gentlemen aren't with me,' she answered, an expression of anxiety taking a firmer hold on her features as she came further into the saloon and the eight men paused just inside the threshold.

They shuffled their feet nervously and waited for one of their number to speak. Edge sipped his drink and muttered:

'From the looks of them, they ain't with me either.'
Then he raised his voice to yell: 'Moses!'

The negro came on the run, and pulled up short in the doorway behind the bar counter. Asked: 'Yes, mister?'

'The lady doesn't touch hard liquor, but she wants a room. These fellers all live around here, so I figure they came in for a drink.'

There was the fresh-faced young preacher, who had taken off his surplice. The slightly-built Stan Barlow who still wore his mourning clothes. The dull-looking Jake Huber. The town blacksmith who was taller by three inches than Edge and broader of shoulder and hips. Two merchants who had not taken off their soiled white aprons. And two men who looked like farmers come to town for supplies.

The blacksmith spat pointedly at the floor, but it was the preacher who spoke. 'We come in friendship, Mr Edge,' he said.

The half-breed took another sip of the whiskey and elevated his glass as he responded: 'I'll drink to that, Reverend. You're all welcome to join me. Long as you pay your own way.'

Anger simmered up behind some of the nervous frowns. The preacher stilled the sounds of it with a gesture of both his hands. Then cleared his throat.

'From what I have heard about you, you are not a stupid man, sir,' he said. 'You are quite aware that we did not come here to drink. Our purpose is two-fold.'

'I'd like a beer, Moses,' Crystal Dickens asked.

And surprise extending to shock showed on some faces as the men watched the Negro fill the order.

The preacher talked over this. 'That very thing is an example of what we have come here to ask you to stop, sir. You and the young lady are both strangers to this part of the country. And strangers from the north. Irving is our town and we ask that visitors here abide by the rules which exist here. Unless the Negro is replaced by a white man, that headstrong young lady will be your only customer.'

'And since this is the only saloon in town, Edge, it likely won't just stop at people not comin' in,' Jake Huber growled and made to push out through the bat-wings.

'Where you goin'?' Barlow asked, voice quavering and brow sweating.

'I told you guys!' the liveryman snapped. 'He's been told all I wanted him to know. I ain't with you on the rest of it.'

Huber went out. But not far. Everyone heard him drop heavily into the bow-back chair on the stoop.

The preacher cleared his throat again. 'There was a shooting in here last evening, Mr Edge. A fine and honest citizen of this town was senselessly killed by a young man who had doubtlessly taken more liquor than was good for him. Tomorrow the culprit will be tried in a court of law. Before a circuit judge and a jury of twelve more fine and honest citizens of Irving.'

'Get to the point, Mr Drabble!' one of the scowling storekeepers insisted.

'Yes, quite so. There were six witnesses, we understand. Three sympathetic to young Warford who will swear the boy fired in self-defence. Mrs Donnelly, who is out of town right now but who intends to return for the trial, will undoubtedly be hostile to the accused. As will this young lady who was the cause of the trouble.'

'I'll tell what I saw,' Crystal said resolutely.

The preacher ignored her to conclude to Edge: 'You, sir, are the only eye-witness totally unprejudiced.'

'Moses there is proof of that, feller,' the half-breed pointed out wryly.

'Shit, there ain't no talkin' to him!' the towering black-smith snarled.

Then caught his breath, as others gasped. All of them, along with the Negro and the woman taken by surprise at the moves Edge made. Rising, whirling, crouching, drawing his Colt and fanning the hammer. The bullets cracked along the saloon on an upward trajectory, the sounds of the rapid firing counterpointed by the tinkle of broken glass and the clatter of falling shards of metal. Then came a stretched second of silence, followed by a crash as the bullet-riddled clock dropped off the wall to the floor.

The half-breed's lean features were impassive as he turned slowly around in the drifting gunsmoke and said evenly to the group of men in the doorway: 'Time's the enemy of all of us. Figure I stopped that clock with the first shot.'

Heavy footfalls beat on the stoop as Crystal added, a little breathlessly: 'That crazy kid fired six at Mr Donnelly.'

'What's all this damn shootin'?' Sheriff Wilde demanded angrily as he barged between the batwings and through the group of men.

'No sweat, feller,' Edge answered as he dropped back into the chair and began to eject the empty shellcases on to the table top. 'Just killing some time.'

Seven

'TRAGEDY and its aftermath are not subjects for black humour, sir!' the Reverend Drabble intoned. 'We have done what we set out to do by coming here. I urge you to take heed of what has been said.'

He swung round and went out. And the others followed: after either glowering at Edge or directing a pleading look at him.

'Mister,' the sheriff said with a weary sigh. 'When I heard that shootin' I sure as hell thought it was the trouble I was expectin'.'

The half-breed finished reloading his Colt and pushed it into the holster. 'Was necessary, feller,' he said, and looked beyond the lawman to where one of Sam Pepper's female guests showed her inquisitive face above the batwings. 'Yes, ma'am?'

'I normally take a drink at noon, young man. I'm given to understand that this is the only establishment in town where I can obtain one. But is it safe?'

'Right now we have the protection of the law, lady,' Edge answered.

'Trouble is they got a black man tendin' bar,' Jake Huber said from the chair on the stoop.

The woman, who was the one who had been travelling alone on the stage, pushed in through the batwings: and revealed the reason for her grimace. 'The entire household staff of my home in San Francisco is Negroid. I'd like a shot glass of Bourbon with some water on the side, if you please.'

'Yes, ma'am,' Moses responded with enthusiasm.

She was tall and thin and expensively dressed in an elegant blue gown: had washed her loose-skinned face and brushed her sparse grey hair since entering the Irving House. There was something regal in the way she walked to a table and sat down, disdainfully surveying the poor quality of her surroundings.

'Why was it necessary, Edge?' Wilde asked after tipping his hat to the elderly newcomer. 'Drabble and that bunch were only here to give you some friendly advice.'

'Excellent service in the circumstances,' the old lady complimented when Moses delivered her order, taking a shot glass of whiskey and a tumbler of water off a wooden tray and setting them down in front of her.

'One time I was butler in a fine house in North Carolina, ma'am,' he answered. 'Before the war that was.'

'So buttle me a rye, Moses,' Wilde growled as he went to stand at the bar beside Crystal Dickens.

'You've changed your damn tune, Wes!' the disgruntled Huber called from outside.

'So go tell the whole town about it, Jake,' the lawman countered. 'Right now my thirst is more powerful than my principles. Well, Edge?'

'Listened to their advice, sheriff. Didn't like it, but listened to it. Fact that my hired help stayed behind the bar made it plain to them how much I didn't like that part of their advice. Decided to blast the clock off the wall as another demonstration. Could've emptied my gun at one of them. But that would've made me as guilty of murder as the Warford kid. Figure that made it plain I don't intend to back up the self-defence plea.'

'I'm with you there, mister,' Huber contributed from outside.

'If you want to stay with me and the rest of the living, feller, best you don't sit in that chair much longer.'

'Uh?' The chair creaked and his feet scuffed the stoop boarding, as Wilde swung away from the bar to eye the half-breed quizzically. Then: 'Hell, Wes!' Huber exclaimed. 'There's a bullet dug into the timber out here.'

'The preacher and his buddies wasted their time,' the half-breed said to the lawman. 'I'd already got the message. And to my mind, bullets speak louder than words.'

'Goodness gracious, and I thought you were drunk,' the old lady said: as Wilde strode out of the saloon to look at the bullet imbedded in the front wall.

'You see who it was?' he called.

'Feller on a hill mile inside the Howling Coyote range.'

'Hal Crowley, it had to be,' Huber rasped.

'Shut your stupid mouth, Jake!' Wilde snarled, and looked grimly in over the batwing doors. To where Edge sat with a quiet smile showing along his mouthline. 'So you heard, mister?'

'Just unwanted advice I'm deaf to, sheriff.'

'Crowley's Joe Love's foreman. Has himself a Sharps rifle with a telescope sight. Rifle shootin' champion of west Texas. I'll go talk to him. If there's any proof, they'll be two cases heard in the court house tomorrow. Anything bad happens to him, there'll still be two cases heard. You understand, mister?'

'Do your job and no sweat, feller.'

Resentment contorted Wilde's neatly moustached features. But he swung away from the saloon doorway and strode angrily away without voicing it.

'Goodness gracious,' the old lady murmured after

emptying her whiskey glass and chasing the liquor with water. 'I was given to understand that Irving was a quiet, trouble-free little town.'

'So it was, lady,' Huber said from out on the stoop. 'Until someone had the guts to stand up against Joe Love. Damn shame it had to be a guy pig-headed about other things.'

He moved off in the wake of Wilde, but more slowly. And the old lady placed a dollar on the table as she stood up.

'Keep the change, boy,' she said as she moved regally toward the door. 'All being well, I shall be back to take my sundown drink this evening.'

'Boy's all right, mister,' Moses said hurriedly while the batwings were flapping in the wake of the old lady's exit. 'It's my skin and I don't mind boy.'

'Here, tip this away,' Crystal told the Negro, pushing the untouched beer toward him. 'I really don't drink. Was just making a point.'

'Obliged,' Edge told her.

'I detest bigotry.'

'Can you cook, feller?'

'Sure can, mister.'

'So go to it,' the half-breed instructed. Then, when the Negro had gone out back, said to the woman: 'There's just the one double room. Last door on the right at the top of the stairs.'

She gasped her shock, then became grim-faced. 'I consider I have paid the family debt, Edge. I asked for a room. And I need no other services, thank you.'

'Suit yourself, lady.'

She gripped her carpetbag, went around behind the counter and through the doorway leading to the back. Her footfalls rapped angrily on the stairs, then were masked by hoofbeats on the street as Sheriff Wilde cantered his horse by. The slamming of a door – not that of the double room – sounded as the lawman demanded a gallop from his mount as he crossed the plank bridge.

Edge rolled and lit a cigarette, listening to the sounds from the kitchen and those of the fast-running stream. After awhile the aroma of cooking food infiltrated into the saloon. This as a group of men came along White Creek Road and entered The Lucky Break. A dozen of them, talking and laughing. Farmers and merchants and clerks. A few of them Edge recognised from his morning trip to the livery. None of them had been with the preacher's delegation.

'Howdy, mister.'

'A man sure gets a dry throat on a day like this.'

'Damn shame about Rusty, but nice someone took over so fast without the place gettin' close at all.'

While some spoke cheerfully to the half-breed, others nodded and smiled in greeting as they all moved across to the bar.

Edge said nothing until he had hefted his gear off the floor and carried it behind the counter. Then yelled through the doorway: 'Moses, we got some thirsty customers!'

'And you've got a hungry roomer,' Crystal said as she reached the foot of the stairs. 'He's fixing lunch.' She brushed past Edge to get behind the bar and asked with a smile: 'What can I get for you gentlemen?'

'Beers. Just beers. And they'll taste real fine after bein' drawn by a pretty little lady like you.'

Edge, as impassive as he had been since the group entered, moved along the hallway toward the kitchen while the other men chorused their agreement with what had been said. He saw that the slices of ham frying in the pan were starting to burn. And he turned them over, because the Negro was not there to do it. Then he slid the Winchester from the boot before he went to the rear door and raked his eyes over the littered back lot and the equally deserted areas out back of the buildings on the south side of Lone Star Street: hooded eyes narrowed against the glare of the afternoon sun – the slivers of blue which showed between the lids glinting like strips of highly polished metal wire.

Then he turned, moved back across the aromatic kitchen and along the passage: into the saloon which was filled with laughter and loud talk and tobacco smoke. The Winchester was canted to his shoulder, but it was as much the coldness of his stare as the slamming down of the rifle barrel on the bartop that curtailed the noise and caused the men to wrench the cigars and cigarettes from their lips.

Several of them held their glasses but there were five on the counter top. And these were sent skidding, toppling, rolling and then shattering to the floor amid their spraying contents as the half-breed swept the Winchester barrel into them.

Crystal vented a choked scream and leapt back, dropping the glass she was in process of filling. This as all but one of the customers lunged away from the front of the bar. The exception was the unfortunate young clerk with ink-stained hands who happened to be standing at the point where Edge released the rifle. Which continued to skitter along the counter under its own momentum then dropped down behind it.

And before it clattered to the floor, the clerk was a trembling prisoner of the half-breed. His coat lapels bunched in Edge's fisted left hand while the right came clear of the hair at the back of the half-breed's head and revealed the straight razor. And finished its forward thrust with the honed blade a fraction of an inch away from the clerk's instinctively closed left eye.

'Jesus Christ Almighty!' a man said shrilly.

'Don't Edge!' the woman implored.

The threatened captive was on the point of passing out, until Edge jerked him forward: up off the floor and folded across the counter.

'Why me?' he whined.

'Luck of the draw, feller,' the half-breed said evenly and distinctly, the words silencing the protests of the other men. Then continued in the same tone: 'Hear tell this is a decent, law-abiding town. Met up with the preacher who should have told all you decent people about some laws that were made before Washington or Austin were ever thought of. This is the one about an eye for an eye.'

'Oh, God,' the clerk groaned. 'What'd I do?'

Edge ignored him to rake his eyes over the shocked faces of the arc of men in back of the helpless captive. 'Clock's busted so you fellers will have to hope my idea of a minute is the same as yours.'

'Edge!' Crystal Dickens pleaded.

'Shut up, lady. A minute is how long you got to bring Moses back here. He ain't back by then, this feller will only see half of what happens next. I'm counting.'

'But mister, we—' a merchant started.

'He's countin', damnit!' a farmer cut in. And led the hurried mass exodus.

Booted feet thudded against the stoop, then on the street. Voices were raised to panic-pitch. Names, among them Drabble, Huber and Marlowe were mixed in with the shrieked explanations of what had happened in the saloon.

Beads of sweat squeezed from the clerk's pores and ran down the trembling flesh of his face. 'Why me, mister?' he blurted again. 'It wasn't my idea to—'

'Guess Moses is thinking along the same lines, feller,' the half-breed rasped. 'It wasn't his idea he should tend bar in this place.'

'Edge, this is making you the same kind they are,' the

woman squeezed out through her fear-constricted face.

'I already told you, lady. I am what I am.'

One pair of running footfalls sounded on the street. Then Moses shouted: 'Mister, mister! They turned me loose! I ain't hurt!'

He staggered up onto the stoop and burst in through the batwings: put both hands on a table and leaned forward, sucking in breath.

Edge slid the razor back in the neck pouch with the same smoothness as he had drawn it. But there was no finesse in the way he dragged the clerk along the shard- and beer-scattered top of the bar counter. Then moved to the doorway, still gripping the hapless man's lapels. Not until he was out on the stoop did he release his grip, and with a nod of the head signalled that the clerk should go to join the group of upwards of fifty men and women gathered at the meeting of Lone Star Street and White Creek Road. A young woman broke free from the throng and ran to meet the clerk, a smile of joy wreathing her tear-streaked face. While those who remained at the corner directed mass malevolence toward the tall, lean half-breed.

'Get outta this town, mister!' the massively-built blacksmith shouted. 'You don't fit in with us or our ways! And if you don't go while you're able, you'll get carried out! 'Cause we wouldn't even want your corpse stinkin' up our cemetery!'

'Quit that kinda talk, Marlowe!' Jake Huber snarled. 'You all right, Rex?'

'Sure, Jake,' the clerk answered, leaning against the woman who had come to meet him. 'Shook up is all.'

'I ain't meanin' that any of us folks will see the stranger gets what's comin' to him, Jake!' Marlowe snarled. 'Be taken care of when the Howlin' Coyote boys come to town!'

Cheers and yells of agreement greeted the blacksmith's words, as the group broke up and moved from sight around the corner.

'I couldn't shout or nothin',' Moses explained over the batwings. 'Come up behind me and put a hand over my mouth. Took me into the back room of Mr Green's grocery store. Mrs Green, she give me a cup of coffee. I knowed they wouldn't hurt me none. Folks here, they ain't got nothin' against me except the colour of my skin. They treat me real good.'

'Long as you sleep in a stable and don't stand too close to whites, uh?' Edge murmured.

'That's right, mister. And that's all right with me. I've had a whole lifetime to get used to things that way and I got used to it. Reckon I'll go finish the cookin' now.'

His tread as he moved across the saloon sounded as morose as his tone.

Then Crystal's face appeared above the batwings, expressing a mixture of anger and sadness. 'Guess he summed it up better than everyone else who's been on at you, Edge. This town may not be perfect, but the people who live here are happy with the way things are. And what right have you to come here and try to change everything?'

'Lady?'

'Yes?'

'If you can't stomach the stink, get out of the latrine.'

'Oh . . . you're as stubborn as a mule and twice as foolish.'

'That could be the point,' he answered pensively. 'For awhile I've come to a fool stop.'

Eight

WORD that Moses had left his job at The Lucky Break saloon spread through town as quickly as earlier turns of events had come to the ear of every interested party.

Probably everyone in Irving knew about it before Edge and Crystal Dickens, who did not find his note until after they had eaten the meal he cooked and took their dirty dishes out to the kitchen.

Mister, you been good to me and you don't deserve no more trouble on account of me. While I was with Mr and Mrs Green, them and lots of other folks said I could work at fetching and carrying for them. Won't pay as good as the work I done for you, but I reckon it will be best for everyone. Moses. P.S. Soon as I got ten dollars, I'll pay you back for the new clothes.'

Neither the half-breed nor the woman said anything after they had read the note. But she sighed and smiled relief while he used the paper on which the message was written to get a light from the stove for his cigarette. Then he went out into the saloon and she washed the dishes before calling that she was going up to her room to sleep for an hour or so. Her tone of voice carried no implied invitation for him to join her and at the top of the stairway she closed her door quietly.

The river rippled and gurgled. Flies buzzed. The timber of the saloon's fabric creaked in the afternoon heat, then again as the cooler air of evening flowed down from the hills of the Howling Coyote range.

It was three hours later, with the light of the setting sun tinged red beyond the shadow it cast of the saloon, when Crystal Dickens came down the stairs and asked sourly:

'None of them had the moral courage to come in yet?'

'Maybe it's just they all drink tea in the afternoon around here.'

'I could use some coffee. You?'

'Obliged.'

Within a few minutes the aroma of freshly brewing coffee infiltrated into the saloon and Edge lit one of the kerosene lamps to shed light on a section of the bar. Was just replacing the chimney when the batwings swung and the aristocratic old lady said:

'Good evening to you, young man. A shot glass of Bourbon with water on the side, if you please.'

'You're a creature of habit, ma'am,' Edge answered as the woman sat in the same chair she had used at noon.

'That I am,' she acknowledged with a sigh. 'But at my time of life the noon and sundown drinking is the only bad one left to me. The boy has gone, I understand.'

'I'll get it,' Crystal offered as she came through the doorway from the rear, and set down two cups of steaming coffee on the bar.

'It won't mean the end of your troubles will it?' the old lady asked as Edge took his coffee to the usual table and Crystal supplied her with her ordered drink. 'You take care in your dealings with Joseph Love, young man.'

'You know him, Mrs . . . ?' Crystal asked from behind the bar where she was sipping her coffee.

'Mortimer, my dear. Winnifred Mortimer of the San Francisco family. I heard of Mr Love from my travelling companions who joined the stage at El Paso. It was not my intention to eavesdrop but within the confines of a moving stage coach when people must shout to be heard, everyone hears. Partners in the meat-canning business, it seems. Hopeful of arranging supplies of beef from Mr Love. But wary. By all accounts, the gentleman is a hard and some say ruthless individual. A bad enemy and an untrustworthy friend.'

'You got an axe to grind, ma'am?' Edge asked.

Mrs Mortimer, who sipped her drink and savoured its taste like it was the last one she was destined to enjoy, shook her head. 'No, young man. I am merely an elderly lady recently widowed. Well provided for with money which my late husband amassed from many enterprises. Beef, mining, railroads and crops. For more years than I care to remember, Arthur and I lived in the lap of luxury while men from the Pacific to the Atlantic shores sweated and suffered and sometimes died to pay for our comforts. Arthur never would bring me to see where our wealth came from. But when he passed on, there was nothing to stop me coming.'

She finished her whiskey and drank half the water before she stood up. 'Those meat men,' she went on as she placed a dollar on the table top. And shifted her intent gaze between Edge and Crystal. 'It could have been Arthur they were talking about. Or many of his friends who he drank and played cards with. Fine, decent men for most of the time. But monsters if the circumstances called for it. And opposition from the wrong quarter was enough to bring out the worst in them. So beware. The richer a man is, the more powerful enemy he makes.'

Slow-moving hooves clopped on the bridge, the horse favouring one of its forelegs.

'I appreciate your concern, Mrs Mortimer,' Crystal said, showed a flickering smile to the old lady and then scowled toward Edge. 'But this gentleman considers himself invincible.'

'San Francisco, New York, west coast, east coast,' the half-breed drawled, pointing a finger at each woman in turn. 'Been there and a lot of places in between. Come up against a lot of rich men. Different kinds, but they all had one thing in common. Not one of them had enough folding green to stop a bullet.'

The old lady smiled.

'That's your answer to every problem, isn't it Edge?' Crystal Dickens flung at him. 'If anyone disagrees with you, hurt him!'

'Such conflicts as these are what I left San Francisco to see,' Mrs Mortimer said, still smiling. 'Good evening to you.'

'What are you staying around to see, lady?' the half-breed asked.

'Justice done,' she answered tersely.

'Edge!' Sheriff Wilde called wearily from the street as the horse was halted.

He rose and went out onto the stoop. A half moon was low in the sky, glitteringly bright and casting long, sharply defined shadows. Wilde had been leading his horse by the rein and both man and animal looked close to exhaustion.

'Threw a shoe halfway between the Howling Coyote ranch house and town.'

'We all have our troubles, feller.'

Wilde spat into the dust. 'Don't invite more than you've got, mister. I talked with Joe Love about the sharpshooter on his property. He agrees that unless some other hot shot rifleman has come to this part of the country, Hal Crowley is the only one could've placed a bullet that close over such a range.'

'Love put up bail for Crowley, too?'

'Crowley ain't around,' Wilde growled. 'He's out line-ridin' somewhere on the Howlin' Coyote. Been gone three days. But hands come and go all the time from the bunkhouse and there's a chance one of them met up with Crowley and told him about the bind Warford's in. Love told me he'll bring Crowley to town if he shows up before they leave for the trial tomorrow. And he will, mister. Joe Love's fixin' to be mad as hell at Crowley if it turns out he did fire that shot.'

'Know how he feels, Sheriff.'

Wilde's weary face became hard-set. 'Like I told you before I took the trouble to ride out to Love's place, mister. I intend for the circuit judge to settle all this. And I ain't about to show fear or favour over who's the accused and who's the witness.'

He realised suddenly that he had lost the half-breed's attention. And he needed to move back alongside his lame horse to be able to peer through a gap in the trees and see what had captured Edge's interest. Four riders cantering their horses along the moon-whitened trail: as yet a half-mile east of the bridge. After watching them for a few moments, the lawman grunted his impatience and growled: 'I'm through givin' out any more warnin's,' then led his horse to the end of the road and around the corner onto Lone Star Street.

'I'll give you one more, Edge,' the blonde woman said coldly over the tops of the batwings. 'Those men heading for town might very well be hired gunslingers.'

He shot an impassive glance over his shoulder at her before returning his gaze to the riders.

'Damn you!' Crystal blurted. 'Aren't you interested in anything but yourself?'

'No, lady,' he answered flatly.

She gasped, then sucked in her breath. 'Well this affects you. While we were down in the funeral parlour waiting for Mr Barlow to get things started, Estelle Donnelly told me what she planned to do with the money from selling this place. She was going to San Antonio to hire men. She's sure that no jury of Irving people will bring in a guilty verdict against Warford. Joseph Love is too rich and powerful, just like Mrs Mortimer said. And if things don't go the way he wants, he'll make others suffer worse than himself. The ordinary people around here, they haven't got the courage to stand up against Love. So Estelle Donnelly plans to see that this time Love doesn't get his own way.'

'Uh, uh,' Edge muttered.

'Don't you see, it's nothing to do with us?' she said with tightly controlled anger. 'All we have to do is tell the court what happened when Warford killed Donnelly and have done with it. We're not on either side and we should have the sense not to get caught in the middle.'

'You hear me tell anyone I planned to do anything else, lady?' the half-breed asked as the four riders slowed their mounts to a walk for the bridge crossing.

'No, no I didn't,' she answered quickly. 'But you don't seem to care who you rub up the wrong way. And in the kind of trouble that's brewing in this town, one wrong word could bring . . . well, let's face it, Edge: you've managed to set everyone against you. So if you need any help, you're going to have a hard time finding it.'

'If you see me looking, lady,' the half-breed said softly, 'you can quit worrying about me. And go see Barlow about burying me.'

'You arrogant sonofabitch!' she snarled at him and whirled away from the batwings to stride angrily across the saloon.

'This the place that used to be called the Red Dog?' one of the strangers asked as all four swung down from their horses.

'You got it,' Edge answered as they hitched the reins to the rail.

They looked like gunmen. All dressed in black from Stetsons to riding boots, wearing short-length coats against the cold of night, hiked up on the right to expose the butts of their holstered revolvers. Men in their late twenties and early thirties with implaccable expressions on their lean, unshaven and dirt-grimed faces. All of them tall and thin with something eager and hungry in their attitudes.

'New owner?' their spokesman asked.

'Two out of three.'

'Two's all I asked, mister.'

'The place is open. You don't want to come in, move your mounts away from my rail. I run a saloon, not a rose garden. So I don't need your horseshit.'

'A hardcase, Curly,' the red-headed and youngest man growled with an evil grin displaying his crooked teeth.

Curly lashed out to the side and hit him hard across the belly with the back of his forearm. Hard enough to force a gasp of pain through the gritted teeth. 'Shut up, Shaft!' he snarled. Then nodded to the half-breed. 'Need rooms. And a little something to wash the trail-dust from our throats. And it sure looks like you could use the business.'

He had stepped up onto the stoop and was looking into the deserted saloon. Edge turned and went through the batwings which flapped closed behind him. From in back of the bar counter, he invited:

'Four of what?'

Curly said: 'Glasses and one bottle of rye whiskey, mister,' as he pushed through the doors and the other three black-clad men followed him. 'You're Edge, right?'

'Four glasses,' the half-breed said, grouping them on the counter. 'And four times right.' He placed an un-corked bottle beside the glasses as the men bellied up to the bar-front and each reached for a glass. 'The Donnelly woman tell you anything else about me but my name?'

Curly drew the cork from the bottle with his teeth and continued to expose them in a grin as he poured whiskey into the glasses. 'Somethin' that Shaft here seems to have forgot, Mr Edge. That you and a gun go together just like kerosene and fire.'

He threw down the drink in one and poured himself another.

Shaft rasped: 'I ain't friggin' scared of nobody with a gun, Curly. Long as I got mine.'

'Somethin' else the mouth here has overlooked. You're with Mrs Donnelly. You figure that cowpuncher oughta be hung for what he did.'

The other three finished their drinks, but waited for Curly to refill the glasses.

'So let's all stay cool, calm and collected,' the group's spokesman advised. 'Ain't no sense in there being any trouble before there needs be.'

'So what the hell we gonna do to fill in the time, Curly?' the man with a livid knife-scar curving down his right cheek growled. 'I had somethin' goin' for me with that little Mex gal in San Antone.'

'The blonde this guy ruffled up when we arrived looked mighty interestin',' the tallest-by-an-inch man added dully, but with a leer twisting his mouthline.

'She for sale?' Curly asked.

'Depends what mood she's in,' Edge answered.

And all five men in the saloon heard the violent sound of the building's rear door being slammed closed.

'Shit, the wrong one,' scar-face muttered.

'So let's play some cards, Reesen,' Curly said, picking up the bottle in his free hand and taking it with his glass to a table. 'All right to light another lamp, Edge?'

The half-breed nodded and Reesen put a match to a lamp-wick before sitting down without enthusiasm at the table with the other three. This as the two meat-canners from El Paso appeared in the doorway.

'That right your help's left?' the shorter and fatter one asked anxiously.

'How can a man's right anythin' be his left?' Curly countered, and followed it with a gust of laughter as he dealt out four hands of cards.

Shaft and the tallest of the quartet grinned. But Reesen scowled as he growled: 'She wasn't in no mood to put out anyway.'

'Moses doesn't work here anymore,' Edge said and the two men on the stoop pushed inside and came to the bar, sending anxious sidelong glances toward the seated gunslingers who were starting a game of five card draw.

'Moses left?' Curly exclaimed. 'Was he sick? Still, maybe he'll get well soon. Long as he keeps takin' the tablets.'

Now Reesen joined the other two in the sycophantic response to Curly's joke.

'Couple of Bourbons,' the taller, elder and almost-bald man from El Paso asked. 'Don't guess you have any ice?'

Again Edge brought up glasses from below the bar, set them on the top and left the customers to open the bottle and pour out their own drinks.

'Of course there's no ice in a place like this, Jonas,' the short, fat meat-canner said after it was obvious Edge did not intend to answer the enquiry.

The half-breed felt ill-at-ease: a sensation he could not recall experiencing for a very long time. Not uneasy in the sense of being afraid. For that was a very familiar feeling, because he knew fear whenever danger threatened – had learned to harness and use such uneasiness so that it honed his reflexes when he moved to combat whatever menaced him.

No, this was an entirely different brand of tension that sprang from the knowledge that he was out of place: standing here behind a bar in the squalid saloon of a small west Texas town, dispensing liquor to wh.)ever happened to come through the batwings. And doing this simple chore badly – aware that he would never impr(ve because he had no wish to be better at it.

In the knowledge, too, that he had known at the star this was how it would be – this morning when Crystal Dickens had tossed the bill of sale on the table and announced it was made out in his name. But he had refused to admit that as a saloon keeper he was doomed to failure – was encouraged in this attitude by the fact that the situation was thrust upon him. He had not sought it for himself.

And it had seemed like a chance to test if he was yet ready to forsake his drifting way of life and settle peacefully in one place. Not necessarily this place, which might serve only as a test.

Which, he acknowledged as he rolled a cigarette, maybe it had. In which case he had failed. Irving was like no other town, but then all towns were different: yet the same to the extent that each had a pattern of life and living to which members of the community adhered. And, as the blonde had pointed out earlier, Edge had succeeded in alienating almost every member of this community. Simply by being himself – which indicated that he was not ready to adapt his code of living to conform with the rules which enabled other people to live close-knittedly together.

Perhaps he had been ready to consider this line of thinking earlier in the day: while he was sitting out on the stoop before he was shot at or when he sat in the saloon and Crystal Dickens was up in her room asleep. But his subconscious had avoided it. Now, without the Negro or the woman to act as his surrogate in the supply of customers' needs, the man named Edge was forced to face up to his failure: as he lit the cigarette and his slitted eyes glinted with hatred in the flare of the match flame.

'All I said was do you mind if we have refills, mister,' the El Paso man called Jonas muttered nervously.

The half-breed looked directly at both men and they backed off a step. Then became rooted to where they stood when Sheriff Wilde yelled:

'Nobody move a muscle!'

The lawman and two others had approached the front of the saloon silently and made no sound as they stepped up on the stoop. But their booted feet came down heavily and the batwings banged hard against the inside walls when they advanced on to the threshold.

Jake Huber flanked Wilde on the left and the massively built Marlowe was on the right. All three men held Colt revolvers which they aimed at the quartet of card-players. The liveryman and the blacksmith wore deputies badges pinned to their vests. All three faces were sweat-sheened. Huber's gun-hand shook.

'What the hell, Sheriff?' Curly asked as the meat-canners turned their heads like they had painfully stiff necks.

Shaft and Reesen twisted from the waist to look toward the doorway: just as slowly but with less tension in their movements. Curly and his tallest partner merely had to look up from their cards to see the newcomers with the levelled guns.

'Yeah, what the frig did we do?' Shaft augmented.

'Shut up, mouth,' Curly said flatly. 'Let's all put up our hands.'

'That's the way,' Wilde urged and now that he was not shouting the strain could be heard in his voice. 'We're here to stop trouble not start any. Like for you boys to spend the night and some of tomorrow with me over at the gaolhouse. Free room and board. And not a stain on your characters when I turn you loose.'

'Oh, my God!' Jonas gasped and dropped his empty glass.

'Sorry about this, gents,' Wilde apologised. 'Disturbance'll be over in a little while. Jerry, go get their guns.'

'Sure thing, Wes,' the blacksmith responded eagerly and advanced into the saloon.

And Edge vented a low sigh which only he and the two men from El Paso heard. Then he spat the cigarette from his lips when he rasped at them: 'Down!' And drew his sixgun.

Jerry Marlowe needed to go around a table to reach the four men with raised hands. And in so doing placed his massively-built frame momentarily in the line of fire from the guns of Wilde and Huber.

Curly and the tall man unfolded to their feet, kicked over the table and started down on to their haunches as if every part of the move was spring-loaded. At the same time as Shaft and Reesen powered sideways off their chairs. The hands of all four men streaked downwards and revolvers were clawed from holsters.

'Watch out!' Wilde shrieked.

This as the two men from El Paso hit the floor hard in response to the half-breed's order. And Jerry Marlowe took two bullets in his chest, was knocked into a half-turn and cork-screwed downwards to flop across a chair that collapsed beneath his weight.

Wilde, and an instant later, Huber, blasted shots across the falling form of the big blacksmith: and Shaft screamed as he was hit in the shoulder – became silent when the second bullet drilled a hole through his forehead above his right eye.

Edge's gun exploded twice in unison with those of the lawman and liveryman. And Curly and the other gunslinger slumped to the side, blood pumping from bullet holes in their heads. Protected by the table from the guns of the crouching Wilde and Huber but exposed on the right flank to the half-breed's Colt.

'All right, all right!' the scar-faced Reesen screamed, powering up and hurling his gun away. 'That's it!'

Fear spread rapidly across his bristled features, displacing the vicious hatred which had contorted them since Curly had signalled the fight to start.

'Easy, Jake,' Wilde rasped as he and the liveryman came erect and he saw the degree of anger which gripped Huber and caused his gun-hand to shake. 'It's over, old buddy.'

'They killed Jerry, Wes,' Huber groaned.

'Take care of that myself,' the big blacksmith forced out through the blood that bubbled in his throat.

'Help me!' Reesen implored, his fear-filled eyes raking from Wilde, to Huber to Edge: as he heard the small sounds which were made by Marlowe moving on the shattered chair.

'He ain't armed!' Wilde yelled. And directed a tacit plea with his wide eyes toward Edge.

Marlowe raised his head and his gun and squeezed the trigger. Firing under a table to send the bullet on an upward trajectory into the crotch of Reesen. Who screamed and stepped backwards, hit the overturned table and slid down it: clutched with both hands at the blood-soaked pants as his legs splayed across the floor.

'She was a Mexican, feller,' Edge said softly.

And drew the uncomprehending stare of the scar-faced man as Wilde lunged forward to try to snatch the smoking gun from Marlowe's rapidly weakening grasp.

'You called the woman you left in San Antonio a Mex,' the half-breed had time to add before the blacksmith managed to thumb back the hammer and squeeze the trigger again.

Wilde was stooping over Marlowe then, free hand clawing toward a broad shoulder. But he was too late and he froze as the gun exploded. To gaze like everyone else at the blood which gouted from the wound opened up in Reesen's throat. For a stretched second while the victim's shocked nervous system held him rigid against the table top – before he became limp, his chin dropped to his chest and he toppled slowly to the side.

Then the lawman wrenched his head round to gaze with smouldering hatred at the half-breed as he rasped: 'You could've shot the gun outta Jerry's hand, mister! Just because that guy used a word you don't like you—'

'Just thought I'd make the point while there was time, feller,' Edge answered as he started to reload the Colt. 'What happened while I was making it was between Marlowe and Reesen.'

'The guy had surrendered and we had him covered!' Wilde snarled. 'It was cold-blooded murder, damnit!'

'Makes it even-steven,' the half-breed said as he holstered the gun and came out from behind the bar.

'Sure does, mister,' Marlowe croaked wetly as the El Paso men got shakily to their feet and parted hurriedly to allow Edge to move between them. Each word he spoke trickled more blood from the corners of his mouth. 'Reckon it ain't often a man gets the chance to kill the one that's killed him. Thanks, mister.'

'Don't talk, Jerry,' Huber urged. 'I'll go get Doc Brady.'

He swung to go through the batwings, the scrape of his bootleather on the floor masking the thud of Marlowe's head against his outstretched right arm.

'He's through talking, Jake,' Wilde reported mournfully as he straightened up. 'Forget Doug Brady. Fetch Stan Barlow.'

'Dear God,' the liveryman breathed, and sagged against the door-frame.

'What is it, Jake?' Sam Pepper called. 'What's the matter now?'

'Jerry's dead, Sam. Shot down by a bunch of hired guns Estelle Donnelly sent to town.'

Huber staggered out through the batwings and the flapping of the doors counterpointed the ugly wet sounds of the liveryman as he vomited on the stoop. Then roars and shrieks of rage from the throats of a large crowd of townspeople filled the night air. And Wilde whirled and strode to the doorway.

'Get on home, you people!' he bellowed. 'It's all over! Ain't nothin' left to do but bury the dead!' Then he lowered his voice to rasp: 'Pull yourself together, Jake. We gotta get this mess cleared up and figure out how to handle things better next time.'

'Robbing the dead is despicable, sir!' Jonas growled, despite the efforts of the shorter and fleshier meat-canner to shush him.

Wilde whirled away from the doorway and expressed greater contempt than ever for the half-breed who was coming up from a crouch.

'They had a bottle of rye they didn't pay for,' Edge said evenly. And opened his right palm to display some coins he had collected from those scattered with playing cards and broken glass when the table was overturned. 'The two-buck debt is paid now.'

'Mister, you're the meanest sonofabitch I ever did lay eyes on,' the sheriff rasped.

'Wes, he likely kept us from endin' up the same as Jerry,' Huber muttered through the kerchief he was using to wipe the vomit off his lips and jaws.

'I sent you to bring Barlow!' the lawman snarled at him.

'Stan was in the crowd outside. He's gone for his wagon.' Huber subdued the rising anger and nodded curtly to Edge. 'Thanks for the help, mister. It was real stupid of Jerry to be so careless. The woman warned us those San Antone people looked like professional guns.'

'Jonas!'

'Freemont!'

The women's shrill voices cut through the tense silence which followed Huber's remarks.

'It's all right!' the taller El Paso man yelled. 'We're all right, Mildred. Can we leave, sheriff?'

The exchange jerked Wilde out of deep and bitter pensiveness. And he looked confused for a few moments until he made sense of the query which had registered in his sub-conscious. Then:

'Sure. Sure, go ahead, gents. I'm sorry you had to be witnesses to the killin's. It ain't usual in this town.'

The meat-canners bobbed their heads and scuttled out: could be heard reassuring their wives that they had survived the gunfight without anything more serious than shaken nerves.

'Guess you can confirm what Miss Dickens said, mister?' Wilde asked Edge. 'Estelle Donnelly hired those men?'

'Right, feller.'

'Four ain't enough,' the lawman said to Huber. 'We got to be ready for others, Jake.'

A wagon and horse could be heard turning the corner and coming along White Creek Road as the liveryman snatched the deputy badge off his coat and held it toward Wilde.

'*You* have to be ready, Wes,' he said dully. 'Because you're the sheriff and it's your job. And Joe Love better be ready because this trouble is between him and Estelle Donnelly.'

'But Jake—'

'I've had enough, Wes,' Huber cut in and waved a hand over the sprawl of bodies around the overturned table and smashed chair. And the star flew out of his trembling fingers. 'When me and Jerry said we'd give you a hand, we didn't expect nothin' like this. And I ain't gonna risk endin' up like poor old Jerry. Not on account of trouble that ain't none of my concern.'

He turned and pushed out through the batwings, as the wagon rolled to a halt and the town's mortician dropped to the stoop.

'It would seem sir,' Barlow said as he entered the saloon and surveyed the carnage, 'that you chose a particularly inappropriate new name for this establishment.'

'How's that, feller?' Edge asked as he went back behind the bar counter.

'Why, The Lucky Break, of course. It would seem that misfortune has attended you since you first set foot on the premises.'

'Same as last night, feller.'

'Pardon?'

'You don't have to haul my carcase down to your funeral parlour,' the half-breed explained.

Barlow frowned, then sighed. 'Well, I suppose that after what has happened, you are entitled to consider yourself lucky to be alive, sir.'

'I work at staying alive. And the harder I work at it, the luckier I seem to get.'

A half-dozen men came into the saloon and were uncomfortably hesistant until Barlow told them to bring blankets from the wagon and wrap the dead in them before taking the bodies outside.

During the exchange with the mortician and while the corpses were being removed, Sheriff Wilde remained detached from his surroundings: deep in anxious thought.

'I'll have the personal effects sent across to your office, Wes,' Barlow said at length. 'Bill the county for burial expenses?'

'Sure, Stan,' Wilde acknowledged absently. Then, when he and Edge were alone: 'Jake was right, mister. I have to thank you. Way things were, you kept him and me from being out on that wagon with Jerry Marlowe. Hasn't none of this mess been of your makin' and you sure as hell didn't have to side with us when the shootin' started.'

'No sweat,' the half-breed said.

Wilde nodded, tight-lipped, and went out of the saloon, his footfalls on the stoop masked by the sounds of the wagon swinging in a tight turn away from the front of The Lucky Break.

'Why did you help him, Edge?' Crystal Dickens asked from the doorway in back of the bar counter.

He finished rolling the cigarette and lit it before he answered: 'I owed him.'

'For what?'

'Buying a drink in here when Moses was tending bar.'

'That was worth risking your life and killing for?'

'It's what I do best, lady.'

She came along behind the bar, went past him and out to the other side. Where she began to straighten up the wreckage where five men had died.

'What the sheriff said about none of this being your making was true, wasn't it?' she muttered at length. 'He couldn't say that to me. Because it's all my fault. If I hadn't been in here last night, Warford wouldn't have had cause to shoot Rusty Donnelly. And it was money I gave her that allowed Mrs Donnelly to hire the gunmen. And me having your name put on the bill of sale meant that you—'

She broke off as the elderly Mrs Mortimer came into the saloon. Then continued: 'Meant that you got involved. And if I hadn't gone to tell the sheriff about those men, Mr Marlowe would still be alive.'

There was a crack in her voice and in the lamplight her eyes were glazed with threatened tears.

'Now, now, my dear,' the old lady said tenderly. 'Life deals us the cards and we play them as we think best at the time.' She lightened her tone. 'What a day it has turned out to be. I feel in need of a nightcap before I retire.'

'Here you are, ma'am,' Edge said, bringing the three-quarters-full bottle of Bourbon up from under the counter. 'Figure Pepper will let you have a glass and some water. Pay for what you've had when you come in tomorrow. I'm closing up now.'

'I'm sure you are wise,' Mrs Mortimer said as she fisted a bony hand around the neck of the bottle. 'You've had a hard day by all accounts. Good night.'

She went out through the batwings and Crystal closed the big double doors and shot the bolts at top and bottom.

'You want me to fix some supper?' the blonde asked, still on the verge of tears.

'That what you came back for? To clean up and cook?'

'I'm renting a room here if you recall.' She lifted the chimney and blew out the lamp Reesen had lit. 'Doing the chores helps to pass the time.'

'Recall the time passed well enough last night,' he said.

'You said you didn't go with whores,' she accused. 'Yet when those men came in you talked of me like I was one. That hurt me, Edge.'

'It killed them.'

'Oh, damn you!' she blurted, and the tears spilled and coursed down her cheeks. She rubbed at the runnels with the backs of her hands. 'Why do you have to be so icy-cold all the time? Why can't you speak a single kind word to people who care for you?'

'Like I told you already, lady' he answered and moved along the bar counter toward the doorway. 'Actions speak louder than words. I figure you came back here for something other than cooking and cleaning. Door of my room won't be locked.'

She sobbed, blurted: 'Oh, how I hate you for what you are!' and sobbed again.

'You've had the invite,' he called down the stairs. 'Up to you. Whether you come or cry off.'

Nine

THE HALF-BREED slept alone in the big double bed and came awake when the first rays of the new day's sun shafted across Howling Coyote range and in through the window of his room. Awoke as always with total recall of where he was and why he was there. And on this bright Texas morning experienced an unfamiliar pang of regret while his mind dwelt for a few moments on the conversation with Crystal Dickens.

Then he got out of bed and made a short survey of the deserted scene beyond the window before he washed up and shaved in cold water poured from the pitcher on the bureau.

It was while he was dressing that his stomach growled its emptiness and he remembered that he had not had any supper the previous night – next was aware of the slight but appetising aromas of boiling coffee and frying bacon which had triggered the response from his belly.

The breakfast smells were much stronger out on the landing and then as he descended the stairway he noticed an absence of other, less pleasant aromas.

'Excellent timing,' Crystal Dickens said as she went by him at the foot of the stairs, carrying a food-laden tray from the kitchen and into the saloon. 'I heard you up and about and thought you'd be hungry.'

Sunlight and fresh morning air filled the saloon, where

both the big doors and the batwings were fastened open and the windows gleamed with recent cleaning. But the blonde woman had not let it rest with the windows. The floor, walls, tables, chairs, bar counter, shelves, glasses and bottles, lamps and even the spittoons had received attention from her. And in her brushing, dusting and polishing she had eradicated every vestige of staleness from the place.

Then had attended to herself so that she looked neater, fresher and prettier than he had ever seen her – the blue denim pants and check shirt she wore detracting not at all from her femininity in the way the fabric closely contoured the curves and hollows of her body.

'You went to a lot of trouble to prove your point,' he said as he sat at the table where she set down the tray.

'What point is that, Mr Edge?' Her tone as she off-loaded the tray of two plates and two cups and two sets of eating utensils was as bustling and impersonal as her manner.

'That you only came back here to cook and clean.' He started to eat.

She sat down opposite him. 'There may have been another reason, Mr Edge. But I prefer to do what I want to do when I want to do it. This place was certainly in sore need of some tidying up and I felt in the mood to undertake it.'

'I'm obliged.'

'You don't have to be. After the trial, you intend to move on don't you?'

'A trial or whatever.'

Her composure was ruffled by anxiety which paid a brief visit to her brown eyes. Then she controlled it. 'Whatever the outcome, you will not remain in Irving. So you will have no use for this place.'

'Guess not.'

'I'd like to buy it off you, Mr Edge.'

'How much?'

'What you paid.'

'Seems fair.'

'You agree?' Now there was surprise in her eyes which showed no sign of last night's weeping.

'Sure.'

She left her breakfast only partially eaten and stood up. 'Good. Now that I won't disturb you, I'll start in to clean the rooms upstairs.'

She turned away from him too quickly for Edge to detect any clue on her face to hint at her true feelings about his acceptance of the deal. But just before she went from sight through the doorway in back of the bar counter he saw a shudder of pent-up emotion ripple the flesh of her back under the shirt. And he finished his breakfast and smoked a cigarette without trying to guess what brand of emotion had triggered the physical response. While he listened to the rippling water of White Creek and the somehow angry banging sounds the woman made as she went about the upstairs cleaning chores.

Then he went out to the stable, saddled his gelding and took the horse for an exercise ride. Away from the back lot of the saloon and the best part of three miles across the dusty semi-desert country to the south of the trail he had followed to reach Irving two nights ago. He galloped, cantered and trotted the animal, which responded eagerly to each demand: obviously delighted to be free of the confines of the stable. Then he veered his mount to the right, reached the trail and headed back to town at an easy walk, hat pulled down low at the front so that the wide brim shaded his eyes from the glare of the morning sun.

It was eight by the clock in the window of Corwin the Druggist when he rode into the midtown area: and Moses was in process of opening up the drugstore, just as doors were being unlatched and window shutters taken down at the front of other business premises along Lone Star Street.

'Reckon you got my note, mister,' the black man called miserably. 'Only done it for the best.'

'No sweat, feller.'

'I got more grave-diggin' chores today. Oughta be able to pay back a couple of dollars come noon.'

'Fine.'

Jake Huber creaked wide the doors of his livery stable and seemed unpleasantly surprised to see the half-breed astride the gelding: turned quickly to go back inside, where Edge glimpsed the horses of two of the dead gunslingers and guessed the other two were also stabled there.

The door of the law office was closed and sun glinting on the window was as effective as a blind from where the half-breed glanced toward it.

People who had yesterday greeted Edge or cast furtive glances at him took pains not to meet his impassive, level gaze this morning. And neither did he sense their eyes at his back after he had ridden past them.

What he did sense was the beginning of uneasiness. And if he felt any response to this, it was nothing more than a calm acknowledgement that he was no longer the major reason for the town's apprehension. Maybe they resented him for the part he had played in priming a potentially explosive situation: but the main cause of their concern was the menacing situation as a whole.

He turned the corner onto White Creek Road and saw close to a dozen horses were hitched to the rail out front of the saloon. And six more were tethered to three of the uprights supporting the awning of the hotel stoop. One of these was the big bay stallion Joseph Love had been riding yesterday. And as Edge dismounted and walked his horse along the line hitched to the saloon rail he saw that each was branded with a pictograph of a coyote in a howling attitude.

The low buzz of conversation from within the saloon was briefly interrupted as he was spotted by the cow-punchers. But was in full swing again as he reached the alley between The Lucky Break and the hotel and Sheriff Wilde yelled:

'Edge!'

The half-breed halted and waited for the lawman to reach him from where he had emerged from the court-house opposite the bridge.

'Just set up things for the trial. Should get started at noon if the eleven o'clock stage runs to schedule. Can rely on you and Miss Dickens being there?'

'Just the one trial, sheriff?'

There were sweat-stains under the armpits of Wilde's cream-coloured suit jacket and he patted at the moisture beads on his forehead with a black handkerchief. 'Joe Love's in the hotel with Warford and a couple more of his hands. Talking business with the two meat-canners from El Paso. I had a word with him before they got started. Hal Crowley hadn't shown up before Joe and his boys left for town.'

Edge spat into the dust of the alley-mouth.

'I believe what he said, mister!' Wilde rasped.

'Fine,' the half-breed responded evenly. 'Need to go see if Crystal wants some help. Seems a trial's good for the saloon business.'

'You know better than that!' the lawman snarled. 'Word reached the Howlin' Coyote about Estelle Donnelly hirin' professional guns. That's the reason why there are so many Love hands here.'

'Who carried the word, feller?'

'My boy Joel,' Sam Pepper announced grimly as he emerged from the hotel, speaking through teeth clenched to a cheroot. 'Because I told him to. Ain't no point in holdin' a trial unless it's fair and free from duress. You ready to go select the jury, Wes?'

'Sure, Sam.'

The men's lack of enthusiasm for the task sounded in their voices and was visible in their gait as they moved toward the meeting of Irving's main street with White Creek Road.

Edge led his horse out to the stable, unsaddled him, checked on the feed and water and when he emerged saw Moses heading for the cemetery in back of the chapel. The Negro was dressed in his old and ragged clothes and there was a shovel canted to his shoulder.

'Hear tell business is real good now I ain't tendin' bar, mister,' Moses said happily.

'Yeah, the lady's been cleaning up, feller,' Edge answered.

'Lady?' Moses asked, perplexed.

'Forget it.'

'All right, mister. But I sure ain't forgettin' about the money I owe you. Two bucks by noon, like I promised.'

'Way things are shaping, you could be clear of debt by soon after that.' The Negro showed perplexity again, until the half-breed explained: 'Looks like there could be a boom in the grave digging business, Moses.'

The black man was abruptly infected with the same brand of apprehension as Edge had seen in the faces of people on Lone Star Street and those of Wes Wilde and Sam Pepper. 'I'll tell you true, mister,' he said. 'I'm real anxious to pay off what I owe, but I'd rather raise the money some other way than digging holes in the cemetery.'

'Guess so, feller,' the half-breed drawled. 'Nobody likes a dead-end job.'

The kitchen he entered as Moses moved off – not chuckling this time – was as spick-and-span as the saloon had been at sunrise. And still was, despite the presence of the dozen or so customers who sat at tables or were aligned along the bar. To an extent, the Howling Coyote hands complemented the impression Crystal Dickens had made on the bar-room with her hard work. For although they were dressed in workclothes, their pants and shirts were freshly laundered and pressed. And all of them were washed up and shaven. And because of their neat and clean turn-out, the majority of the cow-punchers looked uncomfortably misplaced as they sipped frugally at their beers – no hard liquor was in evidence – and directed challenging glances at Edge when he showed behind the bar: their eyes seeming to invite him to do or say something which they might claim as provocation to reveal they were not the dude ranch-hands they obviously considered they appeared to be.

Just as when he had led his horse across the front of the saloon, the talk was momentarily halted. But then was taken up again: with beef, cattle drives to the north, old spreads they had worked and women they had known providing the subject matter for most of the conversations.

'You know, Mr Edge, I think I could really get to enjoy this line of work,' Crystal Dickens said, her tone of voice and her expression showing relief after the brief period of tension had elapsed without trouble.

'Everyone ought to do what they like,' he answered, conscious of being watched surreptitiously. And track-ing down the interested parties to a table at the rear of the saloon – the trio of men who had witnessed the shooting of Rusty Donnelly by Dean Warford. They were not talking. Instead, shifting their eyes to stare morosely down into their untouched glasses of beer when the half-breed looked toward them.

'I think everything's going to be all right,' the blonde said, lowering her voice to ensure that the four men standing to the bar could not overhear her. 'There are fifteen men from the ranch here – not counting Love and Warford. All of them armed.'

Edge had noted the Winchester rifles in the boots hung from the saddles on the horses out front. And seen that every man in the saloon wore a handgun in a holster.

'Then there's the sheriff and however many people he can deputise,' Crystal went on eagerly. 'Mrs Donnelly would have to hire a whole army of men to risk—'

'Your average cowpuncher,' Edge cut in quietly, 'only ever fires a gun into the air to keep a herd on the move. And the only living thing he ever hurts is a steer when he ropes and brands him.'

'I don't know about that,' she came back, her enthusiasm only slightly diminished. 'They look really tough to me.'

She raked her admiring eyes over the customers.

'They are tough,' the half-breed allowed, rolling his second cigarette of the day. 'They have to be to do their job. And they know how to do those jobs. Different line of work to the trade Curly and his partners were in.'

Crystal frowned, then brightened. 'Those men are being buried this morning, in case you've forgotten.'

Edge nodded. 'They got careless, lady. Any more of their kind ride in, they'll expect to find the first four. When they don't, they'll learn by the mistakes the dead men made.'

Now the woman sought to bolster her flagging morale with a harshness of tone that emphasised her actual disbelief in the words she rasped. 'Well, I think you're wrong. I think that if more of the kind who were in here last night come to town, they won't dare to cause trouble.'

'And Dean Warford will walk out of the courthouse a free man.'

'If he does, then it'll be because a jury brought in a verdict of not guilty. And I'll go along with that because there's nothing I can do about it.'

She stared up into the pale blue slits of his eyes, her own challenging him to fault her reasoning. Edge said nothing – merely shifted his gaze away from her face to rake it over the bunch of Howling Coyote men before looking impassively back at her again.

She expressed defiance. And shook her head. 'I don't believe a jury would be intimidated by these men. You've just said they haven't got what it takes to harm hardened gunmen. So they're hardly likely to . . . why, they're neighbours and probably some of them are friends of the men who'll be on the jury.'

'Easy, lady,' Edge murmured as her face grew flushed and her tone became harsh again. 'You got this started. For nothing as far as I'm concerned. What happens in this town and who makes it happen doesn't matter to me. I'm only here to give evidence at the trial. I don't live here anymore.'

'But you do,' she protested. 'Until I pay you, you still own this place.'

'Riders comin', boys!' a man who had risen from a table and gone to look out over the batwings announced.

'I already sold it to you,' Edge told the woman as the rest of the customers went to check on what the cow-puncher at the doorway had reported. 'Over breakfast.'

'But I said I'd give you what you paid for it. Five thousand dollars. It's not mine until I've—'

'What I paid for it was nothing, lady,' he corrected. 'And I agreed for you to have it for the same.'

'But—'

'Lady!' Edge growled. 'I told you right at the start the money in your brother's bank account was never mine.'

He pushed past her, went out through the end of the bar and to the nearest window. To watch, along with the Howling Coyote hands, a bunch of six or so riders approaching Irving on the east trail. They were still a long way off and could be seen as no more than a dark patch against the dust-cloud that was formed of motes kicked up by the cantering hooves of their mounts.

'Somebody better go tell Mr Love we got company comin',' a cowpuncher said flatly.

And the man who had first seen the riders went out through the batwings and along the stoop toward the hotel. This as Crystal Dickens moved up alongside Edge. Close enough for him to feel the spasm on his arm as her shoulder trembled.

'Dear God, why did I have to find out about the money in Mason's account,' she murmured. 'Or stayed in the east and enjoyed it. Already six men have died because of it.'

'Sure did turn out this time that honesty wasn't the best policy,' the half-breed answered as he dropped his cigarette and stepped on it with a boot heel. And added: 'Make that seven, lady.'

This as the bunch of cowpunchers in the doorway vented their surprise with gasps and low-voiced curses.

'What is it?' the woman demanded, squinting in the sunlight shafting through the newly cleaned window.

'Somebody else's number just came up,' Edge supplied, raking his eyes away from the suddenly halted group of riders to locate the last vestiges of a puff of white muzzle-smoke before the vapour disappeared against the backdrop of rolling countryside north of the trail.

'You mean . . . oh no!'

She covered her ears against distant gunfire and screwed her eyes tight closed to blot out the indistinct view of what was happening on the trail.

Another long-range shot had been exploded from the hills and a horse had gone down: was left where it lay as riders urged their mounts into gallops, exploding rifle-shots wildly in the general direction from which the opening gunfire had come.

'Six, seven, eight . . .' Crystal Dickens moaned. 'Please let there be no more.'

Edge rasped in response: 'Lady, don't count on it.'

Ten

EDGE left The Lucky Break Saloon by the kitchen door while the shooting-out on the east trail continued to occupy the attention of the Howling Coyote hands and to keep Crystal Dickens intent upon blotting from her hearing and sight everything that was happening around her.

It was ended by the time the gelding was saddled and he led the horse out of the stable and swung up into the saddle. Hoofbeats and raised voices replaced the sounds of gunshots in the hot morning air as the half-breed rode on a diagonal line from the rear of the saloon into a gap between two of the old adobe buildings on the south side of Lone Star Street.

He crossed the broad, tree-lined street at the same easy pace he had done everything since turning away from the window in the saloon. And was seen by only a few women clutching their children and the more timid male citizens of Irving: for the majority of the town's population had been drawn on the run to the corner where they could gaze fearfully toward the cause of the shooting.

Then he went between the dry goods store and the mission church where work on renovation had been temporarily interrupted, and left town on the trail that snaked north-eastwards.

He did not look backwards at any time as he followed

the trail for half a mile to where it began to parallel the course of the stream in a wide sweep around the base of a hill. Where he crossed the fast-running water. On foot, leading the gelding by the reins and testing each step carefully. White Creek was about sixty feet wide at this point, but Edge had to cover half this distance again as he veered to left and right and avoided water any deeper than waist level.

And before he had ridden another half-mile, almost to the crest of the hill, his pants had dried to an uncomfortable stiffness in the morning sun. As he came close to the brush-covered ridge he was able to see the scattering of farms to the north. Maybe a dozen of them in a valley with the rapidly narrowing stream meandering along the bottom. Nothing bigger than twenty acres. All with creek frontage and each property separated from its neighbours by wire-strand fencing. Small houses with at least one out-building apiece, surrounded by fields cropping cotton, corn and melons.

Smoke rose from a few chimneys and here and there a man or woman worked in the fields. But most of the valley's population seemed to be aboard the two flatbed wagons which were rolling slowly down the trail toward Irving.

Across the stream from the farms, a scattering of cattle grazed the open rangeland.

Edge merely glanced at the peaceful pastoral scene as he swung down from his horse, sliding the Winchester from the boot: aware that he had probably been seen by the people on the wagons even though they were still the best part of two miles away.

Then he moved with the gelding out of their view – up and over the crest. From where he could see just the treetops and the roofs of some of the buildings of Irving above the ridge of an intervening hill. But he had not come out into the rolling range of the Howling Coyote spread to view the town: glanced at the rooftops and trees only briefly to check his bearings. Then led his horse down the hill's eastern slope, along a gulley where his approach put to flight a bunch of twenty or so Long-horns, and up a steep grassy bank dotted with immature Alligator Junipers.

Close to the top of the bank he tethered the gelding's reins to one of the shrub-high trees and only then became aware of the greasiness of the palm of his right hand fisted around the frame of the Winchester. The sweat of tension erupted by the possibility that the sharpshooter may well have changed his position after bush-wacking the horsemen on the trail: and could have aligned his telescopic rifle sight on the half-breed at any moment.

Still sweating, still directing frequent glances to his left, Edge climbed to the very top of the bank, covering the final few feet on his belly. Where he looked through the spiked foliage of a juniper and allowed his thin lips to curl back in a grim smile.

Hal Crowley had not moved away from the vantage point where he shot at the men on the trail. That it was the Howling Coyote foreman there could be no doubt, for the half-breed looked down upon the man over a distance of no more than sixty feet. And at that range he could recognise the lines of the .50 calibre Sharps buffalo gun with a ten-power telescope mounted on the barrel.

He was a tall, cadaverous looking man in his forties with short-cropped black hair, a prominent nose and a thin moustache. Dressed in a brown shirt and pants with a grey Stetson hanging down his back. Edge saw him in profile, seated on a flat rock behind a clump of six-feet-high buttonbushes that concealed him from the trail, where a horse lay dead, a half-mile beyond. The rifle was resting across his thighs and he was playing a bored game of pitch and catch with a pebble that arced monotonously from one hand to the other. And each time the stone was in the air he cast a glance away from it: looking over the angled buffalo sticks and through the foliage of the buttonbushes at the trail. He was humming tunelessly. Then abruptly became silent and allowed the pebble to fall to the ground: as he stared fixedly ahead.

Edge glanced in the direction where something had attracted Crowley's attention: and saw that three more riders were heading toward Irving from the east – had cantered into view from out of the fold of two hills. Then movement closer at hand drew his narrow-eyed gaze back to the Howling Coyote foreman. Who rose from the rock to go down on one knee behind the bushes, nestling the barrel of the Sharps in the vee of the buffalo sticks and pressing his right cheek to the stock of the rifle.

The half-breed, with a much closer target than Crowley's, needed only his left hand under the barrel to steady his aim through the Juniper. And the muzzle wavered hardly at all in the part of the second it took to pump the action of the Winchester.

Crowley moved his thin cheek away from the stock of the Sharps as the only sign that he had heard the un-mistakable series of metallic sounds of a bullet being jacked into the breech of a repeater.

'Let go of the gun, stand up and turn around, feller,' Edge instructed flatly. 'Or drop down on the other knee and pray.'

'I'm not a believer,' the man answered, no quiver of fear in his voice.

'Believe me,' the half-breed urged. 'Or in a very short while you'll find out if you were wrong about the other feller who claims that vengeance is His.'

'You're Edge,' Crowley said as he allowed the stock of the Sharps to fall – the barrel still resting on the buffalo sticks – came to his feet and turned around. He elevated his arms slightly from the elbows so that his hands were at chest-high and forward: the right one at least eighteen inches away from the butt of his holstered Remington sixgun.

The half-breed rose, too, and aimed the Winchester from the hip as he pushed between the Junipers and started down the slope.

'The scope of your knowledge doesn't impress me, feller,' Edge told him.

Crowley was a fatalist, so that as the half-breed came closer to him and he could see the cruel set of the thin mouth and the ice-cold glint in the slitted eyes, his attitude did not alter. A man had got the drop on him and what kind he was didn't matter. He was maybe afraid of dying, but not of the instrument of his demise.

'On the Howling Coyote we look after our own, Mr Edge,' the lean-bodied and thin-faced man said levelly. 'When I heard you was aiming to see young Dean Warford hang, I did what I do best to try to stop you.'

'When it's said a man did his best, the talk is about a loser,' Edge countered as he came to a halt at the foot of the slope, a short spit away from Crowley.

'Didn't get a chance at you until the afternoon. Sun hit the lens in the telescope, I figure.' He shrugged. 'In the morning with the sun behind me . . .?'

'You did fine this morning,' Edge pointed out with a movement of his head.

Crowley turned his emotionless gaze toward the south, where the three riders were moving at a gallop after pausing to check out the dead horse.

'Got one of them plumb through the side of the head,' he said. 'Rearing horse took the second bullet. Dumb luck. Good for one of them, bad for me.'

'You heard the Donnelly woman was hiring on professional guns?'

'Right, Mr Edge. And you're not going to ask me how

I knew those guys were it? Instead of cowpokes, drummers, Texas Rangers or eastern dudes come west to gawp at us natives? Reckon you're the kind that knows the difference well as me.'

'Figured you ain't always been a cattleman, feller.'

A dull light of nostalgia entered the dark eyes of Crowley and he sighed. 'Started out as one on the family spread up in Wyoming. Then come the war. Always was a hotshot with a rifle. Killed me a good few Yankees with a scope rifle. Perry long-gun it was in those days. Guess you was a Yankee?'

'Was. But that has nothing to do with this. Just an American, like you.'

Crowley nodded his acknowledgement that he was due to die out of a grudge of recent origin. Then: 'After the war was lost I did a little hell-raising. Ran with outlaws. Got my ass in a sling and could have put my head in a noose if I didn't join the other side. So was a Ranger for awhile. Until all the rules and regulations got me down. Worse than the army. Hired on with Mr Love then. That's my life story, Mr Edge. Looks like you're the only one who'll know my death one.'

'Your boss tell you to bushwhack me and the Donnelly guns, feller?'

Crowley pursed his lips and shook his head. 'Oh no, Mr Edge. Joseph Love is not the kind of man to order killings. It was a bunch of the boys who rode out to find me and tell me what happened in the Red Dog. About you being the big witness who was likely to get Dean Warford hung. And the same bunch that told me how mad Mr Love was when he found out about the shot I took at you. And that hard men were heading into town.'

'You figured to pick them all off one at a time from up here?' the half-breed asked.

The tall, thin man shrugged his narrow shoulders

again. 'Enough of them to scare others away. Handguns aren't my style, Mr Edge. I'm not going to draw against you. So you'll have to blast me in cold blood.'

'No sweat, feller. Figure you had to be icy calm to fire at me from near a mile away. One other thing before you have to go.'

'What's that?'

'If your boss is so full of the milk of human kindness, why are Irving folks so shit-scared of him?'

'Well, I'll tell you,' Crowley started to answer.

And went for his gun.

A move the half-breed had been expecting ever since he called him to surrender. Because it seemed obvious that Crowley's icy calm indifference to his fate was a fake. The man had been around a long time and in many dangerous situations. And still had a great deal of life expectancy if he could call upon his experience of past tight corners to escape this one.

So, while appearing as outwardly nonchalant as the other man, Edge was constantly poised to respond to Crowley's inevitable move. But was surprised by the nature of the action.

For the man did not reach for the holstered Remington. Instead, hurled himself backwards. Into and through the buttonbushes. Reaching for, grasping and lifting the Sharps as he threw himself past the angled buffalo sticks. And for part of a second the mind of the half-breed was filled with the image of a man named Adam Steele. Another man who had taken a long-range shot at him and missed. And who rated his rifle so much higher than a revolver that he did not even carry a handgun.

Then Edge took two forward steps, the muzzle of the Winchester still trained upon Crowley as the ranch foreman struggled to bring the Sharps to bear from where he lay on his side among the bushes.

But it was neither the repeater nor the buffalo gun that cracked out a shot. Instead a Frontier Colt that was a perfect match for the revolver in the half-breed's holster. This one in the fisted right hand of Joseph Love. Who was in a half-crouch on the far, lower side of the vegetation in which Crowley lay. Dressed in the same stylish attire as yesterday except that the ten-gallon hat had been replaced with a Stetson. And wearing on his distinguishedly handsome face an expression of depthless anguish as he saw his bullet blast a hole in the scalp beneath his foreman's short-cropped hair. A hole that gouted a great splash of dark crimson as the head flopped to the ground after the body had become limp.

'If you still want to know, sir, I'll tell you,' the rancher said as he tossed the smoking revolver into the bushes and raised his grief-stricken gaze from the corpse to the half-breed.

Edge eased the rifle hammer gently forward as he released his hold on the barrel and canted the rifle to his shoulder. His lean features continued to display a look of dark and evil menace as he countered:

'You didn't do me a favour, mister.'

Aware now that the instant during which the half-breed might have killed him was past, Love was staring fixedly down at the corpse.

'He said you take care of your own around here,' Edge went on. 'Make it a point to take care of my own wherever I am – trouble.'

Love wrenched his head up and showed that anger was struggling against grief for command of his features. 'So let another man take care of this, stranger!' he snarled. 'Or go to hell after you've sent me there! I had more respect and admiration for Hal Crowley than anyone I've ever met or heard of! From Jesus Christ himself to Robert E. Lee! But the crazy fool screwed me up worse than I've ever been screwed up in my life! And since I got the chance to put him where he belongs on account of that, I wasn't about to let some hard-nosed, hard-talking, smart-assed drifter with a fast trigger finger do the job for me!'

Red patches showed through the tan of Love's cheeks and he sprayed spittle as he flung out the harsh words. Then, the emotion expended, he looked suddenly exhausted and much older than his years.

'Hell, Edge,' he growled and rubbed his brow with the fingertips of both hands. 'I got no reason to be mad at you.'

'Maybe I should be grateful for that,' the half-breed murmured, feeling his own cold rage contract into a tight ball at the pit of his stomach. 'The way the feller you were mad at ended up blowing his top.' He spat into a buttonbush as he turned to go for his horse. And added: 'A little disappointment has to be better than a hole in the head.'

Eleven

'IT'S not so much that Irving people are afraid of me like mice are scared of a barn owl, Mr Edge,' Joseph Love said suddenly after a long silence. 'It's just that all of us people around here have a good thing going. Nobody wants to upset the way things are and they sort of look to me to maintain what's called the status quo.'

They were almost at the trail, having walked down from the patch of buttonbushes where Hal Crowley had died. The corpse was now slumped over the saddle of the gelding which Edge was leading by the bridle: needing to reach back on occasion to keep it from sliding to the ground.

They were the first words either man had spoken since the rancher told the half-breed he had come out of town on foot, and asked if he would help bring the body to Irving.

'You know what I mean?'

'And the price they pay is to let your hands get away with murder?' Edge responded as they turned on to the trail a quarter mile east of the bridge over White Creek.

'No!' Love came back quickly and angrily. Then sighed and shook his head slowly. 'There never was a killing in Irving until Dean shot Rusty Donnelly. Trouble sometimes. After a round-up or when the boys got back from a drive to the north. Hard drinking and some fighting. That happens in cow towns. Men who work with cattle don't get to let their hair down very often. And when they do, it can get out of hand.

'But I always took care of it. Paid for the damage. And the doctor bills of anyone who didn't work for me and happened to get caught up in the hell raising. Then there was one time – early last year – when there was a shooting. In front of the mission on Lone Star Street. One of my boys, too falling down drunk to know what he was doing, pulled a gun and put a hole in the belly of a young farmer from north of town.

'Only time we ever had a trial in the courthouse that wasn't over some stupid property dispute or small time thievery. Well, Mr Edge, I let it be known that it could all be sorted out, same as always, without all that legal paraphernalia. The shot boy was going to live and I offered a big chunk of money by way of compensation. But his father wanted more. One hell of a lot more. Majority opinion was that the farming people should have taken my money. And when it came to the trial they made it known how they felt by bringing in a not guilty verdict.'

'What value did you put on Estelle Donnelly's son's life, feller?'

They were almost at the bridge now and Love pulled up sharply and whirled toward Edge. 'Listen, mister!' he snapped. 'I didn't approach that woman! There's no amount of money can compensate a mother for the loss of her son! I told you yesterday! In this case, justice has to be seen to be done! And that's what I wanted! It wasn't me who took off to San Antone to hire gunslingers! And you heard from Hal's own lips that I had nothing to do with having him try to kill you! Or sharp-shoot at the men Estelle Donnelly brought to town! That's why I had to kill Crowley myself, for God's sake! What he was doing was as bad as what she is! And he was doing it in my name! People have to know that I put a stop to it!'

'They can't hear you from here,' Edge said, and started forward across the bridge.

Love moved up on the other side of the corpse-burdened gelding as the organ began to sound in the chapel. Then, after the opening notes, the inexpert playing of Joel Pepper was all but drowned by massed voices singing the sombre lines of 'Abide With Me'. Enough voices to suggest that a large proportion of Irving's population were packed into the small chapel. Outside of which were parked the flower-decked glass-sided hearse and a flatbed wagon. The casket had been removed from the hearse but four plain pine boxes remained on the wagon.

The men from the Howling Coyote were not among the congregation paying last respects to the town's blacksmith. But they had left the saloon and now they filed out of the Cattlemen's Association building to gaze silently at Love, Edge and the limp corpse of Crowley slumped over the gelding.

Mostly there was sadness in the men's eyes. Here and there anger. Some emnity. Dean Warford looked afraid.

'Glad you men did what I told you and quit drinking,' Love said as he held up a hand to signal Edge to halt. Then gripped the corpse under the armpits and hauled it clear of the saddle: carried it in both arms to the rear of the hearse and eased it inside with as much dignity as he was able to muster.

Edge started forward with the horse again, sensing the ill-feeling in some of the eyes that raked after him. Which was drawn away immediately when the rancher revealed:

'I reached Hal in time to kill him before Edge could.'

There were some small sounds of shock against the background of mournfully singing voices. Then:

'So that's it, sir!' one of the cowpunchers said flatly. 'We're pullin' outta town.'

'You're what?'

'There are already nine hard men here, sir. Itchin' to hit back after five of their kind been killed. We held a meetin'. And we agreed we weren't gonna risk our skins if Hal wasn't with us. Hell, Mr Love, he was the only one of us who'd ever been up against pro guns before!'

'If you leave Irving, you don't work for me anymore!' Love warned grimly.

'We took into acount you'd feel that way, sir.'

Edge had come to a stop at the mouth of the alley between the hotel and the saloon, where the mounts of the Howling Coyote hands were still hitched. And was dividing his implaccable attention between the exchange taking place out front of the building housing the Cattlemen's Association and the line of silent men which had formed across White Creek Road where it met Lone Star Street. Youngish, hard-eyed men in sombre-hued attire who carried sixguns in holsters tied down to their thighs. Some smoking, others faintly smiling, a couple licking their lips in eager anticipation, one chewing a wad of tobacco. Nine in all.

'And Dean?' Love asked.

'The bastards are tossin' me to the wolves!' the youngster yelled in a half-snarl, half-moan.

And his voice sounded exceptionally loud in the stillness that enveloped the town as the hymn-singing came to an abrupt end.

'So be it then,' Love said wearily, and just, as had happened after he shot Crowley, the rancher looked very old. 'You men ought to know that if you'd tried to take the boy with you, it would have been over my dead body.' he nodded along the street. 'Not on account of those fastguns Estelle Donnelly hired.' Now he looked toward the chapel, where the door had opened and the mourners were emerging. 'For them. Who wouldn't be burying another of their own if the boy hadn't lost his head.'

The preacher was first out of the chapel. Then Wilde, Huber, Sam Pepper and a fourth pall-bearer with the casket on their shoulders. Next a black-veiled widow supported by two other women. Then a double line of men, women and children. All of whom ignored the scene on the street until Stan Barlow broke from the group to go to his hearse for something. And saw the corpse of Crowley sprawled inside. And yelled:

'Dear God, another dead man!'

Then other voices were raised and the majority of the mourners broke from the solemn procession which had turned to go along the side of the chapel to reach the cemetery out back. This as the Howling Coyote hands with the exception of Warford moved to their horses, unhitched them and mounted, the hired gunmen sauntered out of sight along Lone Star Street, Edge led the gelding down the alley toward the stable and the westbound stage rolled into distant view.

By the time the half-breed had tended to his horse the hoofbeats of the cowpunchers' mounts had faded from earshot and all voices save one were silent. It was Joseph Love who was speaking, explaining in grim tones how it had been necessary to kill Crowley so that Warford could be fairly tried without threat of further bloodshed.

There was coffee in a pot on the stove in the kitchen and Edge poured himself a cup and carried it through into the saloon. Where Crystal Dickens and Mrs Mortimer sat at a table, the younger woman drinking coffee and the older one with her usual Bourbon and water on the side.

'You started early today, ma'am,' Edge said, remaining behind the bar counter.

'Be in court at midday, son,' she answered. 'Reckon the judge won't allow any hard liquor in there.'

Crystal expressed her irritation with the exchange and

rose to go to the batwings so that she could better hear what Love was telling the townspeople. And reached the saloon doorway just as the two El Paso meat-canners and their wives hurried by.

'Running scared they are,' the old lady said scornfully. 'No sense of adventure. Aim to be aboard the stage and long gone before anything happens around here.'

'Maybe you should do the same thing, ma'am,' Edge answered.

She took a swallow of her drink. 'Nonsense, young man. I am an innocent bystander. Denied excitement all my life. And I am not involved in the trouble here.'

'When bullets start to fly, they don't have any minds of their own,' the half-breed drawled. 'And if you take a stray one in the belly you won't get very excited about it.'

The stage rattled over the bridge and rolled along White Creek Road, made the turn onto Lone Star Street. And there was no more talk from Joseph Love. He had said what he had to say and the crowd which had listened to him began to disperse.

The blonde in the sexually alluring pants and shirt turned from the batwings, a smile on her lips. 'It seems as though Mrs Mortimer and all of us are safe. There will be no trouble in Irving. And there need never have been any had Mr Love made his intentions clear from the start.'

'Reckon I'll stay anyway,' the old lady said, and finished her drink. Got to her feet and added: 'I'll see you young folks in court.'

She swept out of the saloon.

'I didn't get a chance to go down to the land office,' Crystal said as she picked up the dirty glasses and coffee cup along with the usual dollar Mrs Mortimer had left on the table. 'Money or not, the papers are still in your name so you're still the owner.'

'Bad investment,' Edge responded with a pointed glance around the customerless saloon.

'Joseph Love ordered his men to stop drinking. And those men from San Antonio didn't set foot in the place.'

'Only fools and cowards drink when they know they've got a gunfight on their hands.'

'So maybe business will pick up now.'

Edge was rolling a cigarette and he said nothing.

Crystal set the dirty things down on the bartop. Hard and angrily. 'At risk of inflating your opinion of yourself still more, I want you to know I was worried about you.'

'Obliged.'

'When Mr Love came in here and we realised you'd gone!' she snapped. 'And he said he thought he knew where and went out of town, too. Then I saw two men bringing in a dead one, I thought . . .'

The batwings flapped under the assault of a light gust of wind. And a flurry of dust blew in under them. The same draught of warm air extinguished the match with which Edge had lit the cigarette.

On a stream of smoke he said: 'So let's close the place and do some screwing, lady.'

'What?'

'Your worry doesn't do anything for me. Your body can.'

Stan Barlow drove his hearse past the saloon and the flatbed followed, Jake Huber holding the team's reins.

'How can any man get as hard as you?' the woman flung at him.

'Guess it must be physical attraction,' he answered.

'I've got to be out of my mind!' she said huskily as she pushed away from the bar counter. 'To give the slightest damn about a man who thinks of me as nothing more than something to empty his lust into!'

She whirled and strode to the doorway, where she turned to hurl at him: 'Let me tell you something, Mr

High and Mighty Edge! The only way you'll ever have me again is by force!'

The doors flapped behind her and before they could come to rest were buffeted again by another gust of north wind.

'What can I do for you, Moses?' Edge asked, sensing a presence behind him and glancing over his shoulder.

'Three dollars, mister,' the Negro said, reaching out to place the bills on the bartop. 'Mr Barlow, he paid me in advance for the two more graves I have to dig. Ain't so certain now that there'll be any more of that kinda work for me.'

'Obliged.' He put the money in a hip pocket.

'You don't mind me sayin' so, mister,' Moses growled. 'You didn't oughta be so mean to that lady. I just couldn't help hearin' what was said between you. Same as I been hearin' other talk this mornin'. On account of most white folks treat a black man like me like I wasn't around.'

'I know you're here and I'm listening feller,' Edge told him.

'Well, mister, I'm here to warn you. From what I've heard, you and the lady are the only friends each of you got around here. On account of the both of you are being blamed for all the bad things that's been happenin' lately. The killin's and them gunmen comin' to town and Mr Love firin' all his hands and like that.'

The half-breed pursed his lips and vented a low sigh as he dropped the partially smoked cigarette into the cooled dregs of his coffee. 'Yeah, Moses,' he said evenly. 'It sure does look like it won't only be the Warford kid who'll have a trying time today.'

'Well, you take care, mister. I can't pay you another four bits if the grave I'm diggin' to earn it is yours.'

He went back through the doorway, into the kitchen and out of the rear door of the building. Just as a crowd of people came around the corner onto White Creek Road and hurried past the newly polished windows and wind-flapping batwings.

Edge saw the sheriff and Sam Pepper flanking a sour-faced old man with a small white pointed beard. Joseph Love, still looking ten years older than he was, alongside the frightened Dean Warford. The obese Estelle Donnelly who had the veil down over her face again. Huber, Barlow, the ink-stained clerk who the half-breed had roughed up the day before and a group of other men who he recognised by sight from passing them on Lone Star Street.

Then Crystal Dickens stepped up onto the saloon stoop, anxiety having displaced the anger on her face.

'Come on,' she said dully. 'It's time to go to court.'

'Sure, lady,' he drawled as he came out from behind the bar. 'That I can do. I just don't seem to be able to pay it.'

Twelve

THERE was a musty smell in the Irving courthouse which bore out what Joseph Love had said about the place being underused. And there were not enough sweating people in there for their body smells to mask the staleness of the atmosphere.

It was purpose-built, the actual courtroom divided into two areas by a wooden railing which stretched from one wall to another three-quarters of the way down its length. The larger section was for those who came to see justice being done and was furnished with twin rows of benches with an aisle down the centre.

The elderly Mrs Mortimer sat alone on the front bench to the right. While on the bench across the aisle were Estelle Donnelly, Crystal Dickens and Edge, directed there by the grim-faced Wilde. The rest of the public section was empty: seemed somehow ominously so in the sunlight which shafted into the courtroom through the three large south-facing windows, its glare reduced by wind-raised dust.

There was a gate in the railing between the benches and beyond this was the area where justice was supposed to be done.

Against the rear wall was the impressive justice bench with a high-backed chair behind it, under two flags pinned to the wall – one the American Stars and Stripes and one showing the Lone Star of the state. The white-bearded judge from San Antonio sat here, watching impatiently as the jury of townspeople and farmers took their places on chairs behind another railing which angled across the corner to his left. Love and Warford sat behind a table which was set parallel to the side-wall on the right of the judge. And Sheriff Wilde stood beside a chair between the judge and jurymen which served as the witness stand.

On the highly polished desk before the judge was a Bible and a gavel: and when the jury had settled themselves, the bearded man used the latter to rap the desk top in a formal call for a silence that was already solid. And nodded to Wilde, who cleared his throat before announcing:

'All right Court of the town of Irving Texas is now in session Judge Warren J. Purvis presidin' over trial of Dean Warford accused of wilfully murderin' Rusty Donnelly in the Red Dog Saloon Irving Texas two nights ago how do you plead boy?'

The sheriff had to suck in a deep breath after blurting out so many words without pause.

'Tell the court, Dean,' Love cued.

Warford swallowed hard. 'I had to shoot Rusty to keep him from blowin' off my head with his shotgun, Mr Wilde.'

'Talk to the judge and call him your honour,' the lawman snapped. 'He pleads not guilty, your honour.'

Estelle Donnelly made small grunting sounds behind her veil.

'Judge Purvis,' Love said as he got to his feet. 'The boy's asked me to defend him.'

'You're no lawyer, Mr Love,' Purvis pointed out in a voice that was surprisingly strong and deep for such a small-of-stature man who was close to seventy.

'I know that. But I know what's fair and what isn't and I want to ask for a delay.'

'You mean an adjournment, Joe,' Wilde corrected.

'On what grounds?' Purvis demanded, showing signs of impatience again.

'That Mrs Donnelly's here along with two other witnesses who are going to say Dean murdered Rusty. But the three men who were going to speak up for Dean have left town.'

'Motion denied!' Purvis snapped. 'It's the responsibility of the respective counsels to ensure the attendance of their witnesses.'

The fat woman sighed behind her veil this time: as Love and Wilde exchanged grim looks and the jurymen's anxiety deepened.

'They cooked that up between them,' Crystal Dickens whispered, leaning close so that her lips were just a fraction of an inch from the half-breed's ear.

'This whole thing seems to be a set-up,' he growled.

'I'd like to ask for an adjournment on different grounds, your honour,' Wilde said.

'State them,' Purvis demanded.

'That the circumstances ain't right for a fair trial. There are gunmen in this town. Hired to come here and influence the way in which the jury—'

'Motion denied!' Purvis cut in.

'Those fellers sure are going through the motions,' Edge muttered.

Purvis glared at him and banged his gavel. 'Silence in court!' he shifted his gaze to Wilde, then treated Love to a look of equal severity. 'I was asked by this town to come here to conduct a murder trial. And I came and that's what I intend to do. Even though the only other time I was here it was a charade and I was forced to sit in judgment over a grave miscarriage of justice.

'As the representative of law and order in this town, Sheriff Wilde, it is your duty to ensure that no duress is brought to bear on the people involved in the trial. I have already informed you, Mr Love, that you are at fault in not having the defence witnesses present. Now you either hold this trial here and now within the laid-down law of the state of Texas or I will put this court into permanent recess. And put in a report to Austin that the town of Irving has placed itself outside the jurisdiction of the state's legal system.'

He banged the gavel again. And glared briefly at every person in the courtroom, including Mrs Mortimer. Then: 'Right, Sheriff. The jury has been elected in the usual manner?'

'Yes, sir,' Wilde answered dully. 'The names were drawn by lot.'

'You have any objections to any of the jurymen, Mr Love? And I warn you I will not entertain objections which smack merely of delaying tactics.'

'They're fine,' Love growled.

Warford clenched his right hand into a fist and chewed on the fleshy part of his forefinger.

Outside, the norther gusted harder, rattling windows and doors: billowing more dust higher to subdue the sunlight with the effectiveness of encroaching storm clouds.

'Call your first witness, Sheriff,' Purvis snapped.

'Take the stand, Mr Edge,' Wilde said grimly.

The half-breed rose from the bench and received an encouraging smile from the old lady as he pushed through the gate in the railing. Crystal Dickens watched him anxiously, the judge eyed him with distaste, and, with the exception of Mrs Donnelly whose face was hidden by the veil, he saw animosity in every other pair of eyes that followed him to the chair.

'Stay standin', take the book in your right hand and repeat the oath after me,' Wilde growled, thrusting the Bible at Edge.

Then, as the half-breed accepted the book, the double

entrance doors of the court burst open and banged violently against the inner walls. Wind-borne dust billowed in and masked the vista of river, bridge, trail and rolling hill-country that would otherwise have been spread beyond the threshold.

A shot exploded.

Edge snarled: 'Know one of my own, feller: sonofabitch!'

Thirteen

BLOOD splashed across Crystal Dickens' left cheek and she screamed. But the sound was of anguish rather than agony. For it was the woman seated next to her who had been hit, the blood spraying out through the fine mesh of her mourning veil. From a wound made by the bullet that entered her neck below the right ear, its impact sending her obese body sprawling to the left.

Eyes which had raked from the abruptly opened doors to the two women now swung back again. And recognised the lanky form and sandy hair of Joel Pepper as the boy with the Winchester still at his shoulder shrieked:

'The bastards have raped Mary-Ann, Pa! Them bastards that fat cow brought to town have stripped her naked and are takin' turns in Mr Green's grocery! Help me! Please help me! No one will—'

'Arrest him!' Purvis bellowed as he banged frantically with the gavel. 'This is total madness! Wilde, go get that man!'

This as Crystal Dickens curtailed her scream and the ashen-faced Sam Pepper led the other jurymen in powering to their feet.

'Leave him be!' the boy's father roared as he shoulder-charged the sheriff who was making an instinctive move to draw his fancy revolver.

Wilde was thrown with a yell against the chair which toppled and tripped him to send him sprawling across the desk: across empty space which a moment before had been occupied by Edge.

Sam Pepper, Jake Huber, a storekeeper and two farmers smashed through the rail gate and raced down the aisle: as Edge reached the rail in front of Crystal Dickens, hooked his hands under her armpits and dragged her bodily across to his side.

'My goodness, this is so exciting!' Mrs Mortimer yelled shrilly. 'Just like I imagined it would be in the Wild West!'

'You're in contempt!' Judge Purvis screamed in competition with the old lady. 'The whole damn lot of you people are in contempt!'

Wilde came painfully erect, shaking his head as if he had been stunned by the fall.

'Move your damn ass, Wes!' Joseph Love yelled, and looked beyond the sheriff to where seven of the jurymen remained static in front of their chairs. 'And you people! This is your frigging town! Your women are out there! Which one of them will be after Mary-Ann Green?'

'Austin will hear about this!' Edge heard the judge shriek ineffectually as the half-breed snatched the chair from behind the grinning Dean Warford. And, one hand fastened tightly around the wrist of Crystal Dickens, hurled it at the nearest window.

The chair sailed through in a shower of glass shards and dust billowed in. He kicked at the jagged pieces remaining in the lower sill and the woman yelled:

'Why, Edge? Why?'

'Because it's frigging safer outside!' he snarled, lifted her bodily from the floor and half-threw her through the broken window.

'I mean why did those men make trouble?' she demanded as he came out after her, both of them cracking their eyes against the gritty bite of the wind-driven dust.

'That's their business!' he snapped at her and took

hold of her wrist again. Started to walk fast along the side of the courthouse and around to the rear as other forms came out of the window.

'That's a stupid answer!' the blonde yelled angrily, breathlessly.

'Their business is trouble, lady!' he growled. 'Don't matter how much they were paid, they came from San Antonio for a fight! And when the town and the Howling Coyote hands backed down from it, they made their own trouble!'

'And us, where are you going? What are we going to do?'

'Get the hell out of here, lady!' he growled as they finished zig-zagging among the tombstones of the cemetery and he started to half-drag her across the back lots of the Cattlemen's Association building and the hotel.

And she began to scream incoherently at him as she staggered: off-balanced because she had brought her right hand across her body to try to pry loose his grip of her left wrist.

'So you run scared, you yellow . . .' She could not think of an epithet or could not bring herself to hurl it at him as they came to a halt on the garbage-littered area out back of the saloon and he let her go. She rubbed her wrist where his clutching hand had bruised it. 'I live here! This is my town! Just like Joe Love said to those men back in the courtroom! And I'm going to do what I can to help drive those evil strangers out of it!'

They stood facing each other with three feet separating them, the norther gusting between the buildings, swirling dust and debris around them.

'You're crazy, lady!' he rasped at her, running the back of a hand over his mouth to wipe the dust off his lips. 'Irving's not worth a damn! It's a nothing town! Wild West for Christ sake, that old biddy called it! It ain't that! And it ain't the law-and-order town people around here tried to pretend it was! It's caught in the middle and in the middle is nowhere!'

'Don't you damn well lecture me to make your excuse for running away!' she raged at him, then lunged around him and into the rear of The Lucky Break. Went through the kitchen, along the passageway and into the bar-room.

This as Edge spat a stream of dust-stained saliva downwind and strode into the stable. Where his gelding turned his head to eye him dolefully as he went to where his gear was stacked in a corner. And slid the Winchester from the boot, took a carton of shells from a saddlebag.

'Later maybe if I live that long,' the half-breed muttered and the horse returned to his feed-box. 'I've got a different kind of riding in mind. Just hope I don't end up dying to get back in the saddle.'

The rear door of the building was banging in the through draught from the batwinged entrance of the saloon. And this masked the sound of Edge's progress through the kitchen – and the voices of two people until he was in the passageway at the foot of the stairs.

'. . . one step closer and I'll shoot you!' Crystal Dickens was saying tautly.

'You ain't got what it takes, lady,' a man challenged with a laugh. 'And all I want is some liquor. Had my fill of what a woman can give a man off that cute little kid down at the grocery store.'

'I'm warning you!' the blonde shrieked.

Then screamed in horror as the half-breed's Winchester cracked a shot through the doorway beside her. And she saw the gunslinger stagger backwards under the impact of the bullet which drilled a neat hole in his shirt-front and left a larger, uglier one as it exited through his back after penetrating his heart. He did not collapse into an untidy heap until he was hit in the back by the wind blown batwings.

'Don't say things you don't mean,' Edge growled as he emerged from the doorway and pumped the action of the Winchester.

'I would have!' she gasped.

'And maybe he'd have believed you if you'd cocked the hammers.'

She stared down with shock widened eyes at Rusty Donnelly's double-barrel shotgun she had snatched from under the counter and hurriedly loaded just before the gunslinger swaggered into the saloon. Then thumbed back the two hammers and snapped: 'Everyone makes mistakes, mister!'

He nodded. 'I've made my fair share these past couple of days. But I figure it's only the fatal one that really counts. Stay here. You saw what the rest of his kind look like. If any more show up, forget you're a woman and keep your mouth shut. Just open up with the shotgun.'

He elected to place a hand on the bartop and swing up and over the counter instead of pushing past her to go through the gap. And reached the flapping doors just as Mrs Mortimer came through them.

'Good gracious!' she gasped when she saw the crumpled corpse with the gory hole in the back.

'We ain't open, ma'am,' Edge told her flatly. 'He just wouldn't take no for an answer.'

'It's all right, Mrs Mortimer,' the blonde behind the bar urged. 'You come in and keep me company.'

The half-breed was outside by then, lips compressed and eyes cracked to glinting slits against the assault of dust and wind. As far as he could see in the limited visibility, White Creek Road was deserted. But he could hear gunfire along Lone Star Street, the shots mixed in with the howl of the norther, the banging of doors and the flapping of store signs on their brackets.

Then he saw a slumped form, half-on the saloon stoop

and half-off at the corner. And a man with his back pressed to the wall. It was Jake Huber who seemed to be transfixed against the front of the saloon, a Colt hanging loosely in his right hand as he stared down at the corpse. Which was recognisable, despite the pool of dusty blood congealing in the right eye-socket, as the remains of Sam Pepper.

'Where are the others?' Edge yelled.

And Huber looked up at him. Blankly for a stretched second. 'Sam,' he croaked. 'Sam was hit as he started around the corner. Joel went crazy. First his girl, then his Pa. He just went out on the street firin' like . . . like I don't know what. Wes told me to stay here. Blast any of them that come this way. Took the others with him. Guess the way Joel was shootin', it covered them.'

'What about all the people who didn't go to the trial, Huber?' the half-breed demanded. 'They giving Wilde a hand in this?'

A shake of the head by the liveryman. 'I don't know, mister. They sure weren't ready for anythin' like this. None of us were. Wes and Joe told us Purvis'd be sure to postpone the trial. Said folks should go about their normal business. The hard men would ride on out with easy money in their pockets and . . . aw hell, what a lousy stinkin' mess.'

A constant barrage of gunfire continued to sound along Lone Star Street. Impossible to discern how many triggers were being squeezed. And the noise of the storm made it difficult to pinpoint the precise positions of the men exploding the shots.

'A mess is what you're making of your job, feller,' Edge snarled at Huber. 'One of the hired guns just got into the saloon.'

The liveryman shook his head. And then his tone of voice was as uncaring as the gesture when he said: 'I didn't see him.'

'And he didn't see you, or you'd be just another fifty cents in the bank for Moses, feller.'

He swung away from Huber who had now taken a firmer grip on the revolver, and ran across White Creek Road to the line of trees on the bank of the stream. Moved through these to the far side of Lone Star Street and then slowed his pace to advance along the sidewalk at the front of a row of stores and offices. A gunsmiths, a milliners, a bank, the land office, a barber's parlour and a photography studio. All of them with their doors firmly closed and the window-blinds drawn.

It was a woman in the hat store who rasped as he passed: 'This is all your doing, stranger. Yours and that slut of a bargirl you live with.'

She was on the other side of the door and Edge did not alter the cadence of his stride as, passing the display window, he jerked the rifle to the side. Held his face in its impassive set as he heard the woman scream in terror to the sound of the big pane shattering under the assault of the Winchester's stockplate. Then, knowing he had continued along the sidewalk, she began to shriek curses after him.

He glanced out across the street and saw a body slumped on the ground amid the swirling dust. Directly opposite the photography studio. One of the farmers who had responded to Sam Pepper's call to action back in the courtroom. He was spread-eagled and prone, with a lot of blood on the back of his suit jacket. More than one bullet had drilled into him and through him.

'Figured you'd run out on us, mister,' Joseph Love growled as Edge reached the end of the sidewalk fronting the frame buildings. And saw the rancher and Dean Warford at the front corner of a derelict adobe house with no roof and crumbling walls.

Love continued to peer diagonally across the street: trying to see through the wind-stirred dust, seeking a target for the Colt fisted in his right hand. Warford crouched behind him, without a gun, and expressed fear of the half-breed.

Although they were close to the area of the shooting, no bullets cracked and thudded about them.

'What I should have done, feller,' Edge answered as he stepped down off the boarding and joined the two men at the side of the crumbling adobe shack. 'Where is everybody?'

'Sounds like the San Antone bunch could still be in Green's grocery,' the rancher answered. 'That's up the street next to the funeral parlour. There's firing into and out of the store, I think.'

'Can't see a friggin' thing on account of this damn dust!' Warford added, no longer afraid of Edge.

'That's the trouble,' Love growled. 'It all happened too damn fast. No way of knowing how many stayed in the grocery and how many came out after the Pepper kid started shooting. And the way our own people are so jittery, they'll likely shoot at anything that moves. Hey—'

A running man appeared amid the swirling grey cloud and the tense rancher brought his gun to bear. Edge swung the Winchester and jerked it upwards as Warford yelled a warning. The barrels of the rifle and the revolver clashed to knock the muzzle of the Colt off target. The sudden unexpected movement caused Love's finger to squeeze the trigger and the revolver exploded a shot into the air.

'Sweet Jesus!' Sheriff Wilde cried as he powered into a dive. And slammed to the ground in the cover of the falling-down building as a fusillade of shots was directed across the street. And bullets added to the dereliction of the weather-crumbled walls.

'See what you mean,' Edge muttered.

'I saw it was him!' Love snarled as Wilde bellied

further into cover before getting to his feet. 'I wouldn't have . . . What gives over there, Wes?'

This as the gunfire was abruptly curtailed. And a burst of raucous laughter competed with the sounds of the dust storm.

'Sheer friggin' murder is what!' the lawman answered. 'There's some of them in the grocery and some in Stan's place. And there ain't enough of us to get near. Sam's dead up at the corner.' He gestured with his Remington toward the centre of the street. 'One of the home-steader's out there. Another one just as dead on the stoop of my office. Charlie Corwin and young Pepper went around to the rear. And they ain't done any shootin' for awhile. So them I don't know about. I left Jake to cover the east end of the street in case any of these people tried to make a break from town. If any did, I don't know if Jake could take care of it.'

'Dead scared is all he is, sheriff,' Edge supplied when the lawman paused to draw breath.

Wilde seemed not to hear him. 'God knows what's happened to the Greens. Dale and Ginny are sure to have put up a fight when those bastards started in on Mary-Ann.'

'And the rest of the fine and decent people of Irving?' the half-breed posed evenly.

'Safe and sound behind their locked doors, mister,' Wilde responded harshly. 'And I don't blame them, either.' He shifted his angry gaze from Edge to Love. Then showed brief contempt for Dean Warford. 'The same way I don't blame the Howlin' Coyote hands for takin' off. Why the hell should they risk endin' up like Sam Pepper and the others on account of trouble that ain't of their makin'?' He spat into the dust eddying around his feet. 'Trouble that was supposed to be settled by due process of law.'

'Well, it wasn't settled that way!' Love snarled. 'And

I'm not so sure I want to put my life on the line for this town where people just hide in their houses while their neighbours are being slaughtered!'

'So get the hell back to the Howlin' Coyote!' Wilde countered in a matching tone. It's my paid job to enforce the law here. And after seein' Jerry Marlowe killed by some of the scum that rode in from San Antone I ain't about to ask anyone else to—'

'I said I'm not so sure, Wes!' Joseph Love cut in. 'That doesn't mean I plan to run out on you. If you have a plan that doesn't sound like suicide, I'll consider it.'

'Me, too, Sheriff,' Warford rasped. 'But I need a gun.'

Edge had been rolling a cigarette during the embittered exchange between the rancher and the lawman. Now, after lighting it in hands cupped to keep the wind from the match flame, he drew his Colt and flipped it toward the youngster. Who caught it with a reflex action of his hands.

'What the hell, Edge?' Wilde snarled. 'He's still under arrest for murder!'

'He shoots fine,' the half-breed answered evenly. 'Maybe a little wasteful with shells is all.'

'And we're being wasteful with time, Wes!' Love snapped. 'While we're hanging around here yakking, those gunslingers could be getting out under cover of all this damn dust!'

Warford scowled as he thrust the revolver into his holster. 'I dunno what come over me in the saloon, Mr Wilde. I just went crazy.'

'Just like the Pepper kid did when he blasted Estelle Donnelly!' Love added shrilly. 'And he's still running around loose with a gun in his hand. Or dead.'

The lawman looked set to argue some more, as he raked his eyes desperately over the faces of the three men who shared the cover of the crumbling adobe house.

'Face it, feller,' Edge said. 'It was a lousy brand of law and order this town had. And now it ain't got any unless you take whatever kind of help is offered.'

Wilde hesitated and the struggle that was taking place in his mind showed on his face. Then, after stretched seconds during which the norther whined and timbers creaked and flapped under its assault, he shook his head. 'No, damnit! We finally got the beginnin's of some regular law and order here. Until the Donnelly woman brought in those sonsofbitches across the street to commit rape and murder. But I'm still committed to bring them to justice the right and proper way. And headin' up a bunch of vigilantes ain't that.'

'Don't be a stupid, stubborn bastard, Wes!' Love snarled. 'How you going to handle a bunch of gun-slingers single-handed?'

Another vigorous shake of the head. 'I ain't. Soon as the first hard men showed up this morning I telegraphed San Antone for the Rangers. Plan on keepin' them in town until the Rangers get to Irving.' A tight grin spread across his face, which he turned full into the wind which cut down the gap between the adobe ruin and the photography studio. 'And I reckon this storm is all the help I need to do that. Them bastards won't dare to ride in it, but it won't stop the Rangers comin'.'

'Mr Edge! Mr Edge! Can you hear me? They've got Miss Dickens and they're burning the saloon!'

The half-breed recognised the voice of Winnifred Mortimer, her shouted words sounding shrill and clear against the storm.

Somebody else heard it, too. Laughed and triggered a shot. Then there was a groan and a thud.

'You crazy lady!' Edge rasped through clenched teeth. And lunged away from the adobe wall and on to the sidewalk, the shouts of Wilde and Love indistinct in his ears.

The elderly woman tourist from San Francisco was slumped on the boarding outside the broken window of the millinery store. She was on her side, knees folded up to her belly, both hands spread across the dark stain on the bodice of her dress.

'Oh, it's you,' she said softly as he dropped to his haunches beside her. She looked shocked, but as yet there was no pain from the bullet in her chest. 'The man with the gun at the corner told me you'd come this way. When I could not find you, I shouted. That was rather foolish, wasn't it?'

Wilde, Love and Warford came to a halt beside where Edge squatted.

'You said they, ma'am,' the half-breed hissed. 'Who are they?'

'Not the strangers. That's why Miss Dickens didn't shoot at them when they came in. Some who were on the jury. And some others I've never seen before. Women as well.'

'Obliged,' Edge said as he rose to his feet. And didn't know if he imagined it or if he actually caught the smell of smoke in the dusty air.

'Easy, mister!' Wilde snapped.

And made to draw his Remington.

Then he and everyone else on the sidewalk froze. Hearing running footfalls on the street. A part of a second later swung their heads to look toward the source of the sound. Saw Crystal Dickens sprinting along the centre of the street. At the same moment she saw them, her terror widened eyes recognising the half-breed. She angled toward where he stood, mouth gaping wide to vent a cry of relief.

Edge lunged off the sidewalk, took three long strides toward her, then hurled himself at her. Terror gripped her face again and sounded in the shrill scream. Which was uttered at the moment of impact.

She went down with a sickening thud and he had to roll to the side in mid-air to keep from crashing on top of her. This as a fusillade of gunshots exploded. And bullets dug divots around them and cracked over them.

The familiar harsh laughter sounded in the wake of the gunfire.

'Edge, they're burning the saloon,' she croaked. 'They blame us for—'

'I already got the message,' he rasped as he rose into a crouch, gripped the neck of her shirt and dragged her to the south side of the street.

She groaned as her bruised body endured more punishment from the wheel-rutted and hoof-patterned surface.

'They hurt you?' he asked as he released her in the gap between two adobe stores.

'Not as much as you,' she growled, sitting up and exploring the small of her back with both hands.

'You rather be dead, lady?'

She looked up at him and became meek under the steady gaze of his ice-cold eyes. 'No, they didn't hurt me at all. They just took Mrs Mortimer and me outside and set fire to the saloon. Let me go after it was well alight. And after telling me how you and I are the cause of all this.' There were tears in her eyes, not caused entirely by pain. And she bit on her lip before saying: 'I'm sorry, Edge.'

'For what?'

'Making you stay here.'

'You didn't make me do anything, lady,' he answered, ripped the cigarette off his bottom lip and tossed it to the wind. 'I'm still around because I made you.'

Fourteen

HOOVES hit hard ground and Edge and Crystal Dickens swung their heads around to look along the gap toward the back lots of the Mexican stores. And the woman sighed when Moses appeared through the swirling dust, leading the half-breed's gelding by the reins. The horse was saddled.

'I couldn't do nothin' to stop them crazy folks burnin' you out,' the Negro said morosely. 'But I got your animal outta the stable, mister.'

'Obliged,' Edge said. And could definitely smell smoke in the air now. Air that was clearing slightly of dust, as the sun showed brighter in the afternoon sky with the lessening in intensity of the norther.

'If you and the lady want to leave, you let me know where I can send it and I'll see you get the money I owes you, mister.'

'Take it in kind, Moses.'

'Uh?'

Edge thrust the Winchester at him and the Negro took it automatically: seemed surprised and then frightened when he realised what he was holding.

'Stay here with her and the horse. Anyone even looks like giving you trouble, shoot them.'

'But—'

'Edge—'

Moses and the woman started their objections at the

same time. Then looked at each other with deep anxiety in their eyes when they realised that the half-breed had left without waiting to hear them: going in the direction from which the Negro had come with the horse.

He was shrouded by the constantly moving dust-cloud before he reached into his hair at the nape of his neck and drew out the straight razor. This as he swung to the right to head west across the back lots of the buildings on the south side of Lone Star Street.

Although visibility was improving, there was still a great deal of eye-stinging dust swirling about his head and he had to feel as much as look for the way toward the rear of the grocery store and funeral parlour. Then allowed himself a tight smile when he picked out the unmistakable shape of the glass-sided hearse which showed that he had reached his objective.

He went down on to his hands and knees then, to crawl under the parked hearse which covered him to within ten feet of the rear wall of the funeral parlour. From where he was able to see what he expected – a man standing on the threshold of the open doorway, gripping a rifle double-handed.

'Reckon the storm'll be blowed out before long,' a man said. Inside the parlour, beyond where the watcher stood in the doorway.

'Sooner the damn better,' another man growled. 'This has been one lousy trip to one lousy town. Faster I'm out of it, better it'll be.'

'Clem won't ever get out of it. Nor Ed, I bet. I reckon he got a different kind of shot than he was after when the stupid bastard went to the saloon.'

'Curly Blake and his partners neither. They sure got more than they bargained for.'

'Bet it was that Shaft character stirred the shit that caused the trouble for Curly. Never did understand why they let him run with them.'

Three men were talking in the funeral parlour. Plus the guard in the doorway. There had been nine hard men aligned on the street when the Howling Coyote hands rode off. Clem was probably the man Hal Crowley sharp-shot out on the trail so he didn't count. Ed had to be subtracted. So that left four. All of them in the grocery? Or all or some of them in the funeral parlour and like the guard not contributing to the sour-toned conversation.

'Jack Savage takes the friggin' cake for shit-stirrin',' the man anxious to leave snarled. 'If that headcase hadn't got the hots for the girl it would've been easy money for us.'

'Quit beefin', Chase. I ain't done anythin' hard here. And neither have you. That was the youngest, tenderest piece of ass I ever had. Sure did a lot to relieve the monotony.'

'Sure enough did,' came enthusiastic agreement.

Savage was not in the funeral parlour and was either the self-appointed or elected leader of the hard men, Edge decided. Both conclusions arrived at from the way the men spoke of him. And the half-breed drew back his thin lips in another tight smile. For this meant he did not have to deal immediately with the smartest member of the group.

Professional gunfighters were, on the whole, not the smartest of men: for it was a stupid trade to be in. And normally they were not herd animals. There were exceptions, such as Curly Blake and his partners. But it was likely that the men who rode into Irving today were individualists. Known to each other, but following the trail from San Antonio in two groups simply because they were all headed in the same direction.

Once in town, all there to do the same job, it had been inevitable that a leader would emerge. Not the hardest of the hard men because by the very nature of their trade, there was only one way to decide who this could be. So the one who, by majority consent, was the smartest. Who, when the assignment went too smoothly for the men eager for action, had correctly judged the temper of the townspeople. And created a little interest.

So far, only the man named Ed had paid the ultimate price. And that as a result of his independent action in splitting from the group to go in search of liquor. While just one man holed up in the funeral parlour was resentful of Jack Savage calling the shots: but he confined himself to voicing his disenchantment with the situation. Was apparently not prepared to do anything more than bemoan it. The inevitable griper that was a part of every group.

And a group was how Edge wanted them to remain, with Savage in control. For, if the leader was taken out or they fragmented for any other reason, the natural cunning that was an integral factor in their trade would come to the surface. And since he could not rely on anyone else in the locked-up and battened-down town to move against the hard men, he preferred to handle them as a single unit following instructions than as scattered individuals acting on their own initiative.

'All quiet out there, Vic?'

'Like it's a friggin' ghost town,' the man in the doorway growled with a glance over his shoulder into the parlour. 'Ain't nothin' out here but the friggin' wind and the friggin' dust. I'm with Chase. Can't wait to get the hell away from this place.'

Then he muttered something softly to himself and Edge tensed to respond when Vic came off the threshold. But he did not come far. A step out, then a swing to the left. Where he halted, leaned his rifle against the wall and used both hands to unfasten the front of his pants.

The half-breed was taken by surprise at the move, but wasted just a second before bellying from under the hearse and rising to his feet. The abating storm masked the sounds of his footfalls, but not the splashing noise of Vic's urine which he directed against the wall.

The man's bladder was only partially emptied when three gunshots exploded in quick succession. Triggered from close by. At the front of the grocery store. And glass-panes shattered. Across the street.

'That's it, let's go!' Chase exclaimed.

Vic cursed as the signal-shots caused him to interrupt the jetting, acrid-smelling water. Then caught his breath when the blade of the straight razor penetrated his skin below the right ear: and in part of a second was driven for its entire length up and into the vital tissues of his head. Edge used his left hand on top of Vic's head to hold the target steady. Then, when the man was a limp corpse, he hooked his left hand under the armpit to keep him erect for the moment it took to withdraw the blade. Which was when the blood spurted in a great, arcing splash.

'Come on, Vic! What the hell you friggin' doin'?'

'Leaking,' Edge rasped softly as he wiped the bloodied blade on Vic's vest before thrusting it back in the neck pouch. Then he transferred the dead man's Colt to his own holster and snatched the Winchester up from where it leaned against the wall. Stepped in front of the open doorway where he knew he would be seen only in blurred silhouette amid the swirling dust.

Just one man saw him. Glimpsed him briefly as he rose from where he had been seated on a coffin and started toward the front of the long, narrow room. Where two others were at the door, which was swinging open.

'San Antone, here we . . .'

The man halted, curtailed what he was exclaiming and started to bring his head around for a double-take at the dust-veiled figure who was taller and leaner than Vic.

Edge pumped the action of the Winchester and

triggered a shot from the hip. Rasped through teeth bared in a killer's grin: 'Tough, feller. You almost died happy.'

Chase took the bullet in his back, for there had not been time for his feet to move and turn the rest of him as far as his head. And he went down like a felled tree under the impact of the bullet which was fired over a range of no more than ten feet.

There was another shell jacked into the repeater's breech by the time the two men at the front doorway whirled to stare across the falling corpse: both clawing for their holstered Colts.

Edge fired again and lunged to the side as another hard man was hit. In the chest. And was forced into an awkward backward stagger through the doorway. Was dead with a punctured heart before he thudded to the sidewalk outside. By which time the survivor of those in the funeral parlour had triggered three shots through the open rear door.

'Savage!'

'You people!' a man roared from the grocery store. 'You better hold your friggin' fire! You hear me? We got us hostages!'

A stack of planed timber had enabled Edge to climb on to the roof of the funeral parlour after he leapt out of the line of fire. And now as he bellied toward the front of the building the gunman's revelation came as no surprise to him. From what Wilde had said, Mary-Ann's parents had been in the store when the men took turns at raping the girl. And during his approach to the funeral parlour Edge had seen no sign of Joel Pepper and Charlie Corwin the druggist who were supposed to have attacked the hard men from the rear.

'It ain't us!' Irving's lawman yelled. 'It's gotta be Edge! He ain't one of us!'

'I don't give a frig who or what the hell the sonofabitch

146

is!' Savage snarled. 'If he fires one more shot, four of your people are gonna get blasted to hell!'

'Show 'em a sample, Jack,' a man growled.

'Yeah, why not,' Savage agreed. 'Outside, kid. And stand by the horses. Run and maybe you'll make it. Your girl and her folks won't. Move your ass!'

Joel Pepper was obviously shoved through the doorway of the grocery store. For his footfalls were fast and heavy on the sidewalk and he almost fell as he plunged down on to the street: his balance further hampered by the fact that his wrists were bound at his back. A length of fabric had been tightly tied at the back of his neck, to hold a wad of something in his mouth

'That's one and we got three more here!' Savage yelled.

'He means it, Edge!' Wilde shrieked 'Joel's out on the street. If you do anythin' to make them—'

'No time for speeches!' Savage cut in. 'We're comin' out and we're ridin' out. That's all anyone needs to know.'

'What about the hostages?' Joseph Love demanded. 'What guarantee you offering that they won't be harmed?'

Another Texas blue norther had blown itself into virtual extinction and now the sun was glaring down out of a cloudless sky again. With just a small eddy of dust rising here and there along the street under the impetus of stray tendrils of breeze that were the death-throes of the storm.

From his prone position in the cover of the roof-sign of Barlow's Funeral Parlour, Edge was able to look along the whole length of the street to where it turned at the timber-lined bank of the stream and became White Creek Road.

Immediately below him was the body of a man who had almost reached the front of the building before several bullets had drilled holes into his chest and torn chunks of flesh off his face. Then, to the right, the carcase of a horse killed in the crossfire. Eight other horses were still on their feet, hitched to the rail out front of the grocery store. Joel Pepper, bound and gagged and trembling stood at the end of the line of horses. Another body was sprawled in the centre of the street. Which meant that Jake Huber was the sole survivor of the jurymen who had rushed from the courtroom after Joel shot Estelle Donnelly.

Doors and windows remained firmly shut and blinded.

Winnifred Mortimer lay in the utter stillness of death on the sidewalk in front of the millinery store's broken window.

Wilde, Love and Warford showed themselves in the gap between the photography studio and the ruined adobe shack. Revolvers drawn but not aimed.

Even over such a distance, Edge could see the beads of sweat on their foreheads gleaming in the harsh sunlight. This as stretched seconds of silence clicked into history and tension seemed to infiltrate a physical presence along Lone Star Street. And black smoke rose in an ominous column from the saloon at the far end.

Then footfalls hit the sidewalk below.

'Hear what I say, Edge!' Wilde yelled. 'You cause any more killin' in this town and you'll hang, so help me!'

The Green family were bound and gagged in the same manner as Joel Pepper. The dazed Mary-Ann wore a torn and tattered white dress and her blonde hair was in disarray after her ordeal. She was no more than seventeen and her parents looked little more than twice her age. Her father had an ugly bruise on his right temple but otherwise he and his wife looked neat and tidy in their storekeeper's aprons.

Edge recognised the girl from seeing her amongst the choir who had peered horrified into the saloon after Rusty Donnelly was killed. And her father as one of those who had come with the town preacher to protest at Moses acting as bartender.

Three of the hard men had revolvers pressed into the backs of the Green family while the fourth unhitched four horses from the rail. Which meant that one had died in the grocery store, his violent end from a bullet fired by a local citizen unknown to the group who had waited in the funeral parlour.

All four survivors shifted their heads constantly to survey the street in both directions. They saw corpses, building façades which showed not a sign that there were watching people behind them, and the trio of men gripping unthreatening revolvers beside the derelict adobe building beyond the mission church.

Mary-Ann and her mother were roughly helped astride horses first, while guns were held to the heads of Joel Pepper and Dale Green. Then, with a rider in the saddle behind each woman, the two men were swung up on to mounts.

'What about this Edge character, Jack?' one of the gunslingers growled. 'We oughta get him out into the friggin' open.'

'No friggin' chance,' the tall, broadly built, Mexican-style moustached Savage answered when he and the other three gunslingers were in their saddles. One hand on the reins and the other pressing a revolver into the necks of the hostages. 'That bastard is like us. And would you show yourself to bastards like us to save the lives of no-account cruds like this?'

There was no response, and Savage raised his voice. 'Right!' We take them across the bridge and then we set them down! Alive! We don't make the bridge, they don't make the bridge!'

He tugged gently on his rein and tapped his spurs lightly into the flanks of his horse. The other three followed his lead.

Slow-moving hooves clopped on the street, puffing up dust.

Nobody in town could hear the thundering of galloping hooves, for the bunch of riders were still too far out along the east trail. And only Edge on the roof of the funeral parlour was in a high enough position to see over the stream-side trees to where the horsemen had ridden around the hump of a distant hill.

It was not possible to foretell if the approach of the Texas Rangers would be heard before Savage and the other hard men reached White Creek Road: or whether they would be seen first. But that was immaterial. Of vital importance – to the hostages – was how their captors would react to what was heard or seen.

The hostages were forced by the gun muzzles pressed to their necks to keep their heads unmoving on their shoulders. While the men holding the guns constantly looked to left and right and behind them.

Edge drew the stolen Colt, cocked the hammer and licked his lips. Showed the killer-grin again when Wilde spoke.

'I'm trustin' you to keep your word, mister!'

The tension that gripped the gunslingers caused all of them to snap their attention toward the sound of the sheriff's voice as they came level with him. Which was the moment when the half-breed hurled the cocked revolver out over the sign and across the street.

His plan depended upon the human instinct that in almost every case places self-preservation above all other considerations.

Thus, when the Colt completed its arcing course and the impact with the front of Huber's livery stable jolted the hammer forward, his sole doubt concerned the response of the dazed and shocked Mary-Ann Green.

The falling revolver exploded its bullet which drilled harmlessly into the ground.

The hard men, Wilde, Love and Warford all swung their eyes to look toward the source of the gunshot.

With nothing to lose if the lead had started to fly, Dale Green and Joel Pepper made their desperate attempts to survive.

Edge had overlooked love as the most powerful impulse in the make-up or some human beings. And vented a non-commital grunt as he came erect with the Winchester to his shoulder – as Green and Pepper flung themselves off the horses. Lunging in the direction that crashed them against the women to knock Ginny and Mary-Ann Green to the ground.

Roars of rage and shrieked curses exploded from throats.

Then a bullet belched from the muzzle of the Winchester. And one of the gunslingers was pitched from his saddle, blood spurting from a hole in his back.

Of Wilde, Love and Warford, the youngster was first to react. Bringing up Edge's Colt and blasting a bullet into the head of Jack Savage as he and the other two men from San Antonio sought to rake their eyes and guns toward the point from where the rifle-shot had come.

But the sheriff and the rancher were only a moment later in triggering their revolvers at the two men in the saddles, whose anger had changed to panic.

Love's shot went high, but as the hard man abandoned his search for Edge and swung to aim at the rancher, Warford and the half-breed fired simultaneously. The revolver bullet took him in the throat and the shell from the rifle entered his heart from the back.

The nervous horses snorted as the final rider thudded to the ground, their nostrils flared to the scents of fresh blood and drifting gunsmoke.

Dean Warford moved forward, gun-hand extended, to check that the four hard men were dead.

This as Crystal Dickens, closely followed by Moses,

ran out onto the street. The Negro to take the reins of the horses and lead them away while the woman dropped into a crouch and worked frantically to free the bonds of Mary-Ann Green. Which spurred Love to holster his gun and go to work on the gag across Ginny Green's mouth.

Wilde, his fancy Remington held loosely in a hand which hung down at his side, watched with something akin to exhaustion in his eyes as Edge swung down on to the sidewalk out front of the funeral parlour.

And the half-breed sensed other eyes upon him as he moved slowly along the street, the Winchester canted to his shoulder. Eyes that hated him surreptitiously through cracks in window blinds.

A glance into the grocery store showed him that Charlie Corwin was not among the watchers. For the town druggist was sprawled on his back with two blood crusted holes in his chest. Close to where a gunslinger was folded over a cracker-barrel, shot by Joel Pepper, the druggist or one of the other townspeople who had been spurred to action by the rape of Mary-Ann Green.

'You got lucky, mister!' Wilde snarled suddenly, as if he had needed a lot of time to gather the strength with which to hurl the words at Edge. 'I meant what I said! You'd have hung for sure if just one more of our people had been killed!'

'Shut your stupid mouth before you regret openin' it, Wes!' Jake Huber shouted as he emerged from the smoke drifting out of the burning saloon.

'You shut yours—'

'The Rangers are comin'!' Huber cut in. 'What chance would the Greens and Joel have had if them San Antone bastards had come up against them?'

'It doesn't matter, Wes,' Love growled as he left Dale Green to help his wife to her feet. This as Crystal Dickens rose when Mary-Ann turned from her to bury her tear streaming face into the crook of Joel Pepper's shoulder: both of them still seated on the ground. 'No point in recriminations.'

The thundering hooves of the horses carrying the Texas Rangers could now be heard in the distance.

'There's going to be worse than just recriminations!' the elderly Judge Purvis cried hoarsely as he hurried after Huber and passed him, rage making the flesh above his white beard almost purple with distended blood vessels. He halted and pointed a shaking arm toward Joel Pepper. 'That boy walked into my courtroom and shot down a witness in cold blood!' He swung his arm and raked his blazing eyes in another direction. 'And just what is that man accused of murder doing with a gun, sheriff?'

'Mine, kid,' Edge said flatly.

Warford nodded, drew the Colt and tossed it to the half-breed. 'Thanks for the loan.'

'No sweat. You killed good this time.' He took the reins of one of the horses from Moses and looked at Crystal Dickens whose face was still smeared with the blood of Mrs Donnelly. 'You want to bring my horse, lady? You can have this one.'

'You're going to ride away from this?' the blonde asked, her voice strained. 'That poor kid's been raped God knows how many times. Warford still has to be tried. The Pepper boy has to be guilty of something. All these dead people . . .'

'We survived, lady,' the half-breed told her. 'What the people who survived here do with the rest of their lives is their business.'

'I want to thank you as well, mister,' Joel Pepper said, looking up over the shoulder of Mary-Ann.

Edge had rolled a cigarette and now he lit it with a match struck on the boot of a dead man. While Mary-Ann's parents looked at him with tacit gratitude in their eyes. Elsewhere, other eyes continued to watch him with anything but gratitude.

'Town was so all-fire sure the lady and me were the cause of the trouble, figured that many people couldn't be wrong,' he said. 'Did what I could to clean up the mess.'

'There are some widows in this town who maybe'll think you left things a little late, mister!' Wilde snarled through his clenched teeth.

'I go along with Jake!' Love growled. 'After I killed Hal Crowley there was no one in the same class as the hard men to go up against them. Except Edge. And if he hadn't done what he did – without anyone asking him – this could have been a lot damn worse.'

Edge checked that Moses had replaced his Winchester in the boot. Then dropped the other rifle and swung up into the saddle of the gelding.

'I didn't make the rules in this place, feller,' he said to Wilde as the blonde climbed astride the stallion of one of the gunslingers. 'Just did what I could to live by most of them while I was here.'

'You two can't leave!' Purvis protested as the group of Texas Rangers slowed their horses on the bridge. 'That young woman is right. You're witnesses in a murder trial. Perhaps more than one trial.'

'We've tried this town,' Edge told the judge flatly. 'And it ain't proved to our liking.'

He heeled his horse forward and did not look back. But heard the clop of the stallion's hooves as Crystal Dickens followed him.

Purvis, Wilde and Love began to yell at each other and the woman brought her horse up alongside the half-breed.

'Thanks, Edge.'

'What for, lady?'

'If I hadn't been in the saloon that night, none of this

154

would've happened. I caused the mess you cleaned up.'

'You don't know me. If you did, you wouldn't be coming with me.' He nodded toward the inert form of the rich old lady from San Francisco. 'West got real wild for her. Maybe because I was around.'

The blonde was morosely silent for a few moments. Then:

'Something you should perhaps know, Edge.'

'What's that?'

'Everything I possessed was in my room at the saloon. That includes the other five thousand dollars. It all went up in smoke.'

He arced his cigarette away. 'Any time it bothers you, lady, think about how much trouble the first five thousand bought.' He turned his head to show her a cold grin. 'Anyway, I figured I'd made it plain I didn't want you for your money.'

They rode around the corner onto White Creek Road, where the dozen young, tall, big-built, trail-dusty Rangers were holding their weary horses to a walk and gazing at the burning remains of the saloon. Part of the front wall was still standing, showing the inappropriate new name which had been inexpertly painted by Moses.

The body of Sam Pepper had been removed from the stoop before the place was put to the torch.

The captain of the Ranger troop halted his men and touched his hat to Crystal Dickens. 'Ma'am. Sir. Trouble is over, I guess?'

'The cavalry usually has the same problem,' Edge muttered.

The captain showed just mild irritation and continued: 'The dust storm held us up from getting here faster. How quiet it is now, sounds like you folks handled things yourselves.'

'Edge took care of it, Captain,' Jake Huber said from the corner before either the half-breed or the woman could respond. His tone was morose. 'And maybe when the people here have time to think things about, they'll realise he deserved better than this.'

He waved a hand toward the burning building.

'This place was yours, sir?' the captain asked with a grimace.

'Lived there for awhile,' Edge answered evenly. 'So maybe I ought to feel honoured.'

'Uh' the captain grunted, he and his men perplexed.

The half-breed was finally able to get the last of the killer-glint from his eyes so that his grin was purely sardonic when he answered: 'The town gave me an illuminated address.'

'Name's Steele.'
'Edge, feller.'
'Sounds like we were made for each other.'
'Maybe, but after you shot my horse,
I ain't so keen on you.'

In TWO OF A KIND, Edge meets Adam Steele.

Now read the Steele series, also by George G. Gilman,
and obtainable from New English Library.

NEL BESTSELLERS

T045528	THE STAND	*Stephen King*	£1.75
T046133	HOW GREEN WAS M.Y VALLEY	*Richard Llewellyn*	£1.00
T060475	I BOUGHT A MOUNTAIN	*Thomas Firbank*	£1.00
T050203	IN THE TEETH OF THE EVIDENCE	*Dorothy L. Sayers*	£1.25
T040925	THE PRIZE	*Irving Wallace*	£1.65
T034755	THE CITADEL	*A J. Cronin*	£1.10
T050777	STRANGER IN A STRANGE LAND	*Robert Heinlein*	£1.75
T050807	79 PARK AVENUE	*Harold Robbins*	£1.75
T042308	DUNE	*Frank Herbert*	£1.50
T045317	THE MOON IS A HARSH MISTRESS	*Robert Heinlein*	£1.25
T050149	THE INHERITORS	*Harold Robbins*	£1.75
T049620	RICH MAN, POOR MAN	*Irwin Shaw*	£1.60
T046710	EDGE 35: TOWN ON TRIAL	*George G. Gilman*	£1.00
T036541	DEVIL'S GUARD	*Robert Elford*	£1.25
T050629	THE RATS	*James Herbert*	£1.25
T050874	CARRIE	*Stephen King*	£1.50
T050610	THE FOG	*James Herbert*	£1.25
T041867	THE MIXED BLESSING	*Helen Van Slyke*	£1.50
T038629	THIN AIR	*Simpson & Burger*	95p
T038602	THE APOCALYPSE	*Jeffrey Konvitz*	95p
T046850	WEB OF EVERYWHERE	*John Brunner*	85p

NEL P.O. BOX 11, FALMOUTH TR10 9EN, CORNWALL

Postage charge:

U.K. Customers. Please allow 30p for the first book plus 15p per copy for each additional book ordered to a maximum charge of £1.29 to cover the cost of postage and packing, in addition to cover price.

B.F.P.O. & Eire. Please allow 30p for the first book plus 15p per copy for the next 8 books, thereafter 6p per book, in addition to cover price.

Overseas Customers. Please allow 50p for the first book plus 15p per copy for each additional book, in addition to cover price.

Please send cheque or postal order (no currency).

Name ....

Address ....

....

Title ....

While every effort is made to keep prices steady, it is sometimes necessary to increase prices at short notice. New English Library reserve the right to show on covers and charge new retail prices which may differ from those advertised in the text or elsewhere.(4)